Ewan Colin Coupar and a
Touch of the Fae

Tae Sasha
"Believe"

Ewan Colin Coupar and a Touch of the Fae

Carl R. Peterson

Illustrations by Kirstin Noel Dorshimer

ISBN-13: 9781539592501
ISBN-10: 1539592502
Library of Congress Control Number: 2016917528
CreateSpace Independent Publishing Platform
North Charleston, South Carolina

Contents

Prologue

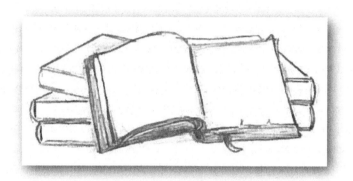

"Come in, come in, Mr. Coupar. Ten o'clock on the dot."

"I'm always on time, Mr. P. It's been important for me to be on time all my life."

"We've read the first six chapters of the story, the first six chapters," said Mr. P., the publisher.

Mr. P.'s name was really Mr. Higginsbottom, but Mr. Coupar somehow could not get his tongue around the word. He called him Mr. P., for publisher, and Higginsbottom didn't seem to mind.

"Actually, you've read six of the first seven chapters. I have chapter one right here." Mr. Coupar put a hefty manuscript on the edge of Mr. P.'s desk.

"Sit down, sit down. Can I get you something to drink? Mmm? Something to drink?"

"Coffee, please, but I'll fix it myself." Mr. Coupar walked over to the coffee table. "If it were ten in the evening, a wee single malt would be nice."

"Then have a seat, have a seat," said Mr. P.

With his coffee, Mr. Coupar sat on a high-backed leather chair facing Mr. P.'s desk.

"So tell me, Mr. Coupar, are you the Ewan Colin Coupar in the story? Is this you as a young chap?"

"Aye, that would be me," said Mr. Coupar.

"Tell me, what exactly is 'a touch of the Fae'? Is it about people who believe in Faeries, or is there more to it than that?"

"It is more than that. You can believe in Faeries and not have a touch of the Fae. You can even see and communicate with Faeries and not have a touch of the Fae. But if you have Faerie ancestries, then you have Faerie blood and so have a touch of the Fae. Understand, though, that lots of folks who have it are not always aware. Unless you develop it, it can be lost."

"Mmm…so we have the first *seven* chapters. Well, we love it. We will publish it, and when your agent arrives, we can go over a proposal. When can we read the rest of it?"

"Oh, it's all here, finished," said Mr. Coupar, putting his hand on the manuscript in front of Mr. P.

"Oh. All of it?" Mr. P. said with a note of concern. "Well, I never expected it to be finished. In fact, I was hoping it wasn't, quite frankly."

"Why is that?"

"Well, I was just wondering if you would be agreeable to a change or two."

"Oh, like what?"

"Well, we love it—we do—but I was wondering if it was movie material. You know, sometimes books like this, fantasies, are great for movie versions. If this took place in England, it might sell better. You know, English accents and all that sort of stuff. Oh, I understand the book just fine, but I was thinking of stories like *Peter Pan* or *Sherlock Holmes and the Hound of the Baskervilles*, *Treasure Island*—by Scottish authors but English settings, you know."

"Aye, maybe, but what about *Braveheart*, *Rob Roy*, and *Local Hero*? They were big movies too," said Mr. Coupar.

"That's true…that's true."

Mr. Coupar didn't say anything about how Mr. P.'s frequent repetition irked him.

"And," Mr. Coupar said, "Would you move the Loch Ness monster into somewhere in England or put the Selkie folk from Scotland in the Thames, maybe? Besides, Scottish Faeries don't like to be English, and, furthermore, it happened in Scotland."

"Well, I agree with some of your points," said Mr. P., "but it *is a fantasy.*"

"Well sort of, I suppose, although I didn't make it up. I just wrote it down the way it happened," Mr. Coupar said.

"The way it happened? Are you trying to tell me it's true, Mr. Coupar?" Mr. P. said with a laugh. "Or is it a Faerie tale, and are you going to start somewhere with 'A long, long time ago' or 'Once upon a time'?"

"Aye, that's what I'm saying, in a sense. You see, by saying 'Once upon a time...' it puts the story in a definite point of time in the infinite. It all happened some time ago but with no particular time that I know of. I know that's hard to explain, but then maybe it's not."

Is this guy loony? I didn't quite understand what he just said but I think I did, thought Mr. P.

"But if it's true, Mr. Coupar, you can take us to the Loch Ness monster or show us Faeries and dragons."

"I can't do that, Mr. P. If you read the rest of the story, you will understand. Go on. Read it."

The book slowly rose by itself, gently dropped in front of Mr. Higginsbottom, and opened at the prologue. Mr. Higginsbottom, with eyes and mouth wide open, started to read.

Prologue

"*Come in, come in, Mr. Coupar. Ten o'clock on the dot.*"

"*I'm always on time, Mr. P. It's been important for me to be on time all my life*"...

In The Beginning

IT WAS SEVEN o'clock in the evening, and night had fallen on this grey town of Greenock in Scotland. It was late autumn, and days were short at this time of year. A solitary figure, that of old Grandpa Coupar, stood in the middle of the railway platform at the West Station. With his hat in his hand, he peered down the tracks. Standing just outside the railway-office door were the porter and ticket master. The sound of the big steam engine pulling its passenger carriages did not seem to come from far away, and in a few minutes its passengers would be standing on the station platform. That would be Grandpa Coupar's son Charles with his three children: Sally, aged ten; Ewan, aged five; and Heather, just three. With them was Charles's sister Kathleen, or Kay for short. All of the children would be celebrating a birthday within the next month, it being the middle of October.

Their journey had started in the seaside town of Westgate on Sea in Kent, England, the day before. After spending the night in London, they continued on the early train to Glasgow. Finally, with a quick change of trains in Glasgow, they rode the last twenty-five miles to Greenock.

Although they had made the trip several times in the past few years, this would be their last. Charles was born in Scotland and was stationed in England as a member of the Royal Air Force during the Second World War. He had married in England but was now in the process of getting a divorce and moving back to Scotland. Many families were torn apart as a result of the war. Many children were left fatherless and many house-wives left as widows. This was not the case with the Coupar family, but after the war Charles longed to return to his native Scotland. That and the fact that Mr. and Mrs. Coupar found themselves somewhat estranged and had drifted apart. So it was reluctantly agreed that divorce was the answer. Charles would return to Greenock where shipyard jobs were plen-tiful and he would carry on a tradition where his father, grandfather, and great grandfather and many others had gone before. Mrs. Coupar would remain in England where she had grown up and continue her career as a nurse. Of the children, two of them, the sisters, were born in England. Ewan, the son, was born in Greenock on one of his mother's rare trips to Scotland to avoid the German bombing raids on London. Kent lay be-tween London and Europe, and the countryside in between was not safe. The children would go with their father to his home with loving and pro-tective grandparents.

The children enjoyed the train ride for most of the way. The English countryside was interesting to Ewan, with hills and valleys, villages, towns, and cities, and much of that was different from city and town living. There were farms and fields with sheep and cows and Gypsy caravans. Charles made the journey interesting by telling the children stories of what they saw from the inside of the passenger cars. They spotted castle ruins and Roman walls, farms and small villages, but Ewan especially liked the Gypsies. Brightly painted horse-drawn Gypsy caravans were common in the English countryside, and they reminded Ewan of the old fellow in *The Wizard of Oz*, a movie they had just seen.

"Will there be Gypsies in Scotland?" Ewan asked.

"Sort of," said Charles, "but they are called tinkers in Scotland, a little bit different."

"Tinkers? What's a tinker?" asked Ewan.

Charles, by this time, was getting weary from storytelling, and night was falling over the countryside as they crossed the Scottish border, so he suggested that it was time for a wee rest and said, "I'll tell ye aboot tinkers later."

Sleep overtook the children for most of the final stage of the trip. Now the journey was almost over—only a few more weary steps to Trafalgar Street. For Charles, it was a pleasure seeing his father waiting for him at the station and knowing that the journey was almost over.

"I'll take the lad," Grandpa Coupar said as Charles and his sister exited the carriage to the platform. Charles handed the still-sleeping Ewan to his father. Aunt Kay carried Heather, who also was sleeping. Sally was groggy but able to walk. Besides, at ten years, she was too big to carry.

"Well, that leaves me to carry the two suitcases," said Charles. Turning to his father, he said, "The rest of our belongings have been shipped. Should arrive in two to three days, I think."

"All right, son. Your mother has moved things around to fit it all in."

The last quarter mile or so was in the cold night air. Ewan, beginning to awake, remembered the big orange lights of Roxburgh Street from the station to Trafalgar Street where Gran was waiting. Roxburgh Street was one of the main streets and was lit by electricity, while most of Greenock's other side streets—as with most of the houses—were still lit by gas lamps. The Coupars' tenement flat on the third floor was dimly lit by a gas mantle, but a fire in the huge black-grate fireplace added warmth and light in the kitchen, something Ewan and his sisters enjoyed on their visits. Now they were here to stay, and their mum was not with them. Charles, Sally, Ewan, and Heather would now be living with Gran and Grandpa Coupar. Aunt Kay, who had taken time off her work to assist with the moving, would soon return to Dunoon to continue her work as manageress for one of the busiest hotels in that Clydeside holiday resort.

One Year Earlier

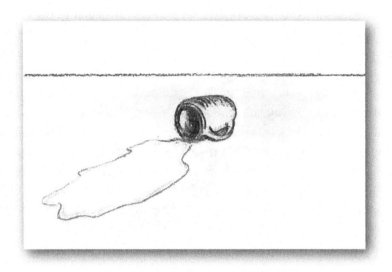

Ewan had been looking out the front living-room window of the house into Adrian Square. Adrian Square was in Westgate on Sea not far from Margate in Kent, a little ways north of the English Channel. The square was nestled between Westgate Bay Avenue and Station Road, and a wee amble down Westgate Bay Road to Sea Road would lead to the beach. Adrian Square was about half the size of a football field, surrounded by a brick wall about four feet high. On each of its four sides was an entrance, and inside the perimeter were bushes of different types, mostly holly. The houses all faced the field. Number eleven, the Coupars' house, was fronted by a smaller brick wall with a wooden gate that opened into a small front garden. It was a split-level house, meaning one could go down steps to a door below or up a short flight of steps to another door above. The inner staircase went up two more levels.

As Ewan looked out the window, a man came through the front gate. "Mum," called Ewan, "there's a man coming!"

The man came to the upper-level door with a bag filled with envelopes and boxes and left a few with Mrs. Coupar. She turned to Ewan. "These are birthday presents for you and Heather, and perhaps for Sally. They're from Daddy."

Their birthdays were all within two weeks from the end of October to the beginning of November. Mr. Coupar was seldom home, it being wartime and he in the Royal Air Force. Sally was attending school at Saint Gregory's, so only Mrs. Coupar was home with Ewan and Heather. Ewan would be starting school soon. Heather was napping, so Mrs. Coupar helped Ewan open his birthday presents. It was a football and football boots, and Ewan could hardly wait to tell Heather and Sally what the postman had brought for his birthday and to see what they would unwrap. It would be some years later before he realized that the presents were not really from the postman but from his father. He had not understood the connection between the two.

The last time Ewan remembered a father was when a handsome young man came to the house for a few days on leave. Ewan tried on this grown-up's uniform, with a hat to match. Everyone seemed happy and liked the young man, but then he was gone again.

When Sally came home from school, she and Heather opened more boxes, but Ewan was interested only in what to do with his own stuff. Sally helped him put on his boots.

"OK," she said, "let's go to the square, and we'll round up some friends and play football."

"I don't know how to play," said a bewildered Ewan. Sally showed him how to set up the goals at each end of the field.

"Now we pick teams," said Sally, "and try to kick the ball into one or the other of the goals, which are these four jumpers and scarves, at each end of the field. We place them about ten feet apart, two at each end, like this."

"OK," said Ewan.

What followed was a bunch of Sally's friends running up and down the field kicking the ball away every time Ewan got close to it. When he finally came to the ball, or it came to him, he grabbed it, took it under his arm, and ran into the house. That was the end of the football game, for nobody could find Ewan after that.

The only other birthday episode Ewan remembered was when he was invited to a friend's party just a few doors down.

"Now, this is for your friend," Mrs. Coupar told him as she gave him something wrapped in a long box. After cakes and drinks and lots of laughing and shouting, his friend opened the present from Ewan.

"Why, it's a cricket set," said his friend's mother. "You can play with this in the square."

The mother set up the wickets, chose teams from the boys and girls at the party, and said, "OK, son, it's your birthday. You can bat first."

"But I gave him the present," Ewan protested. "I should bat first." Ewan grabbed the bat.

"No, it's not your birthday," the boy's mother said as she took the bat away from Ewan. She was about to hand it back to her son when Ewan snatched the wickets, ball, and bat and ran back to his house.

"I can't understand what gets into him sometimes," said Mrs. Coupar. "Always has to be The Boss. Maybe it's because he's in between two sisters. Who knows?"

The situation was straightened out, and everyone had a good time. Ewan, thinking back, would often blush at how stupid he had been at times.

Another incident clear in his mind from those days was one of Captain Brown. The Brown family lived on the same side as the Coupars on Adrian Square. Mr. Brown was a sea captain, strong, stocky, and with a beard. Ewan saw the pirate in him—no patch, though. He was not home much. That was the way it would be with a sea captain. The Browns were a family of five daughters ranging in age from two to nine. One of them, Janet, was Ewan's age. At that age, it was OK to play with girls without being teased about it. It was that sunny day when Ewan dropped by the Brown house to inquire if Janet could come out to play. She said she could, but she told him to wait in the kitchen while she went to her room to change into play clothes. Ewan walked into the kitchen, which had a big round table in the center and chairs around it. Ewan sat down and noticed some dishes on the table, cups included.

Leftover breakfast dishes, Ewan thought. Out of the corner of his eye, he saw a paper being held up with hands holding each edge. It was lowered slightly until the captain's head was visible.

"Good morning, young man," said the captain.

Ewan, taken completely by surprise, stammered something unintelligible. The captain made him nervous at the best of times. *I suppose when you're the boss, you have to be like that*, thought Ewan, *like teachers*. The silence that followed seemed to intensify until Ewan, able to distract himself, watched a fly buzzing around. Ewan's attention focused on the fly as it landed on the table. His hand went out slowly to one of the nearest cups. *I will trap this fly if I can turn over the cup before it moves*. Ewan did his best to overcome his unease in the presence of the captain. To Ewan's surprise, the cup was half filled with milk and emptied over the table. The last thing Ewan remembered was the startled look on the captain's face as Ewan bolted for the front door. Then a funny thing happened. As Ewan ran away, he wished that he hadn't been so clumsy and that he could reverse the accident. Captain Brown tried to utter something at the fleeing boy, and Mrs. Brown came in to see what the commotion was all about.

"Did you see that? He just emptied a cup of milk all over the table and ran out the door," Captain Brown said.

"I see no spilled milk," said Mrs. Brown.

Captain Brown turned around to see the cup in its upright position still half filled with milk. The fly was still buzzing around. With a puzzled look on his face, Captain Brown tugged on his beard, and to this day, the poor man would never have guessed what happened.

Ewan was never aware of what had transpired and was careful to avoid Captain Brown for quite some time. He was surprised that nobody ever brought it up.

CHAPTER THREE

Aeroplane Ride

ONE MORE MEMORY stuck with Ewan for quite some time. It was an event that happened after the war ended, and Mr. Coupar had come home to reacquaint himself with his children. The Coupar family spent the immediate postwar years in a seaside resort of Westgate on Sea before returning to Scotland. Ewan and his elder sister were born during the war years, and both reacted to the goings-on after peace was declared. Folks hearing the sound of a plane would turn their eyes skyward and say, "It's all right. It's one of ours."

During the war years, the enemy planes crossed the English Channel on their way to bomb London and other parts of the country. It was an anxious time. Even after the war was over, it was only natural to look apprehensively toward the skies.

One day, Ewan and Sally were walking along the Esplanade, a tarmac path that ran between the Sea Road and the shore, when an RAF plane flew low and parallel to the shore. There were no furtive stares or "It's one of ours." Nobody but Ewan seemed to notice it. Nevertheless, he felt safe enough to wave to the pilot in his domed but open cockpit. It was a single-front-engine plane, dark green with blue, white, and red circles underneath double wings. The head sticking out of the cockpit wore a leather hat and goggles, and the tails of a white silk scarf floated gracefully behind him. Ewan ran ahead of his sister in an effort to keep up with the plane and possibly converse with the pilot, who had waved back.

"Hello, hello, can I ride with you?" he called.

A bold question, but the pilot looked friendly. He responded by turning around and flying lower. Ewan knew it was coming back for him. Nobody else seemed to be paying attention to the low-flying plane. Ewan made a couple of happy high skips, and after a mighty leap found himself sitting beside the pilot. They climbed higher. Ewan waved to his sister and frowned for just a second when she didn't respond. The noise of the engine and the wind made conversation difficult, but the pilot did convey to Ewan the need to don some goggles. He then explained the scenery below: the English Channel, the cliffs of Dover, and France in the distance. On the English side, small towns dotted the coastline with a number of single dwellings and farms farther inland. The pilot explained that what he was seeing was thirty years before Ewan's time and that things hadn't changed much. Not even the recent war would have significantly changed this part of the country. It wasn't clear to Ewan just what the pilot meant, and Ewan, being only four years old, hadn't been told about a lot of things. The thought crossed his mind to ask his father about this when he got home. If they flew higher, maybe they could see things even farther back in time. The pilot's name was Peter Conway, and he let Ewan know that he was welcome to take more rides if their paths crossed again.

"Just look up when you hear me, and shout 'hello.' I'm sure we'll meet again."

After a few more friendly words with Peter, Ewan found himself back beside his sister.

"Well, that was fun," he said to Sally. "How long was I gone? It couldn't have been too long."

Chapter Three

Sally had moved no farther along the path.

"What do you mean?" said Sally.

"My aeroplane ride, just now. Why didn't you come? There was room, you know."

"What aeroplane ride? When? You've been right here all along. I wish I had your imagination."

Charles listened to every detail about the trip and was impressed, but Sally insisted that no such thing happened. *Maybe she was jealous*, Ewan thought. He would make sure Sally came along on the next trip. Charles couldn't explain right away and said, "We all have different things happen to us."

Such were some of the memories Ewan Colin Coupar would leave behind in England. He had not even thought about what to look forward to in the place of his birth, almost five years ago. To say he had unusual qualities would be true, but nobody noticed them yet, not even Ewan himself. Scotland would unveil just who Ewan Colin Coupar was and what unusual talents or gifts he had.

Twelve Trafalgar Street

TWELVE TRAFALGAR STREET, in Greenock, was a tenement building that was four stories high with two flats each on the second, third, and fourth floors. An Italian confectionary and ice-cream shop were on the ground level. The building stood on the corner of Trafalgar Street and Roxburgh Street. Although the entrance to the flats was on Trafalgar Street, the entrance to the ice-cream shop was on Roxburgh Street. On one of the other corners stood a wee tin church run by the Salvation Army. Directly across from the ice-cream shop on Roxburgh Street was a newsagent store or "paper shop," as the locals called it. Above the newsagent was the Foresters' Hall, which almost every Friday and Saturday evenings hosted weddings, dances, and so forth. It was during those nights that Ewan first heard live music from bands and singers.

Windows from all the flats faced north and south. Gran and Grandpa Coupar lived on the third floor, and the River Clyde was clear from the kitchen window.

The River Clyde starts from an area known as Lead Hills and increases in size as it make its way over a series of falls, the Falls of Clyde, on its way to Glasgow, Port Glasgow, and Greenock. There, it reaches the Tail of the Bank as the river merges into the Firth of Clyde and beyond. It eventually joins up with the Irish Sea. Ships of all sizes sailed up and down the river. In the distance, on the other side of the river, the hills and the mountains of the Highlands were visible. Being so close to the Highlands, Greenock was often referred to as the "Gateway to the Highlands."

This now was the home of the Coupars. Small as it was—with a kitchen, a living room, and one bedroom—it didn't seem crowded for six people. There was a box bed in the wall in the kitchen for Gran and Grandpa, a box bed in the living room for Ewan, a pullout sofa for Mr. Coupar, and the bedroom for Sally and Heather. Two fireplaces, one in the living room and one in the kitchen, warmed the house. The kitchen fireplace was where Gran did all the cooking. All around it were ovens and stove plates. The kitchen also had one sink with one tap and cold running water. Oh, and one thing more: one street block away were all the shops—the butcher, baker, fish shop, pharmacy, and shoes and clothing stores. The school was also close—four blocks to be exact.

"Do they have school up here, Gran?" Ewan moaned when Gran mentioned starting school in a day or two.

"Oh aye, you and Sally will go to the Mearns Street School."

Ewan had attended one year of school in England. Saint Gregory's was a wee semiprivate school, and he had mixed feelings about the experience. He had his first crush, a slightly older schoolmate. To attract her attention, he had run around the schoolyard and fallen in front of her. She had come over to see that he was not hurt. That was the way he got to meet her. The meeting had been brief, so he tried again. It worked with less effect the second time. By the fourth time, she completely ignored him. He liked the school uniforms colored red and yellow and was wondering if his new school would have uniforms.

"What about Heather, then?" he asked.

"Well, she's not quite old enough. Next year, she will go."

Mearns Street School was one of the oldest schools still in use in Greenock. It was almost at the foot of one of Greenock's most visible landmarks, the Whin Hill.

"You'll meet lots of friends there," Gran assured him. "You'll have to wear a uniform too, just like your old school in England. Things'll be a wee bit different tae start wi', but you'll do just fine."

Things were certainly a wee bit different but not in totally unexpected ways. New students were always subjected to a certain amount of scrutiny especially if their accent was different. This made switching from an English semiprivate school to a Scottish public school a daunting experience. But children do have a way of handling these situations, as we will see.

Grandpa folded the paper he was reading across his knee. He then took his pipe out of his pocket and stuck it into his mouth before putting some tobacco in his hand. From the dark lump about the size of a matchbox, he used his penknife to cut off little shreds. He then shredded the tobacco between his palms into smaller pieces before putting it into his pipe and lighting it. This would fascinate Ewan, who would see this ritual many times. Something that would take ten to fifteen minutes to do produced only three to five minutes of puffing. But during those five minutes of puffing, Grandpa would blow smoke rings, sometimes blowing one through the other.

"Dae ye no see the Faeries jumping through the rings, son? That's why I do that—so they can play."

"I think I do," said Ewan, watching stray wisps of smoke floating away, imagining that they must be the Faeries. "Where do Faeries come from, Grandpa, and where do they go after they disappear like that?"

"Och, laddie, they're everywhere. They live in Faerieland mostly, but they like tae hang around just tae see what we're doing. Look, there's one now," Grandpa said quickly as he looked behind a kettle on the grate close to the fire.

Chapter Four

Ewan shot a glance at the fireplace but once again saw only a whiff of smoke from the fire. *That must have been it*, he thought. "Will it not be burned so close to the fire?"

"No, not that kind. Some like the fires tae keep warm. They'll be the ones known as Wag-by-the-Ways."

"What others are there, Grandpa?"

"Well, laddie, there's Brownies. They like tae help folk wi' chores around the house."

"Aye, we could be doing wi' one of them anytime soon," chirped in Gran.

"And then there's Goblins," Grandpa said.

"Oh, I like those ones the best," said Sally, suddenly getting into the conversation.

"What do you know about Goblins?" asked Gran.

"Well, once when we came up to Scotland before for a visit, Dad took us up the cut for a walk, and there are lots in the woods up there."

The cut was a series of aqueducts that had been cut into the hillsides behind Greenock to bring water from a man-made loch, known as Loch Thom, into the town. It was now a favorite area for Sunday afternoon walks and picnics.

"How dae ye ken that?" said Gran.

"Well, I saw them, of course," said Sally, "and they tried to scare me, but they didn't, you know. I tried to catch one, and he seemed surprised, you know."

"Oh boy!" Now Ewan was excited. "Can we go up there again and capture one?"

"Maybe," said Sally.

Nobody noticed the surprised look Gran shot to Grandpa. "Ach well, back tae the first day of school," Gran said to change the subject.

"But if it's just to have friends, Gran, you said there were lots living around here," Ewan said.

"Aye, but they all go tae school as well. There would be nobody to play with if ye didnae go, and forby that you have tae learn tae read and write and do arithmetic. We have to make smart weans of all of ye, ye ken."

Ewan sighed and then whispered, "Gran?"

"Yes son?"

"Are there really such things as Faeries?"

"What kind of question is that? Did Grandpa not just tell ye?" Gran wondered why Ewan would ask such a thing out of the blue. "Of course there is."

"Have you seen any?"

"Aye, och, it's a long story. I'll tell ye later." She wondered just what she would tell Ewan later.

Before Sally could disappear to attend to her homework and other such chores, Ewan caught up with her to ask about the Goblins.

"Sally, did you really see Goblins up the cut?"

"Yes, well, they're just like wee people about three feet high, if that. I think they're all related to one another in some way—the Leprechauns and Brownies and Dwarves. They are very elusive, though."

"What does that mean?" asked Ewan.

"Hard to catch, I suppose. I remember once when I was chasing them, all of a sudden a big Faerie appeared in front of me and told me to stop bothering them. She was tall and slender and beautiful with long white hair, although she looked young. She had on a lovely long silken green dress that hid her feet. She moved toward me slowly, taking small steps. Then her dress changed to pink. I was a bit scared now, but she told me not to be afraid and that her name was Pinto. But as she came to me very dainty-like, I think she tripped on the hem of her dress and came tumbling down on the grass, rolling over and over. Very undignified. I thought it was very funny and started to giggle, and when she got up she was very angry with me. She glared at me, as if to say it wasn't nice to laugh. Then she just disappeared. I haven't seen her since."

"Are you pulling my leg? Is that really true, and you're not making it up?" asked Ewan.

"No, it's true, cross my heart. There are lots more interesting things up here than in England. Ask Grandpa about the Wee Cheenie man, and ask Gran about that big rock she visits in Gourock."

Chapter Four

Sally explained that she had heard Grandpa talking to a Wee Cheenie man who was his friend. He would sometimes visit the old man's hut in the Well Park and at times would walk with him to and from the park.

"Have you seen him?" asked Ewan.

"No, but I've heard them talk. I think he's a wee Goblin. Wouldn't be surprised," said Sally. "And have you noticed when Gran goes to Gourock, she always goes to the same spot and talks to a big rock that she likes to sit near?"

"I did notice that, but Gran talks to herself a lot."

"Don't be too sure it's to herself," Sally said and left it at that.

CHAPTER FIVE

A Different Place

THIS WAS GOING to be an experience for Ewan, for he was now living in a much different place. He was fairly sheltered from outside life at Adrian Square, and his friends were children who lived roundabout the square. The children he was about to meet from the neighborhood and from his new school would be prone to teasing newcomers, especially ones with English accents and no knowledge of street life in Greenock.

Ewan was fortunate, however, to have a cousin one year younger who took it upon himself to look after Ewan—for a while, at least. Jim lived less than half a mile from Ewan and was Gran's sister's grandson. That actually made them second cousins, but who's counting? Jim was rather amused about how little Ewan knew about things that everybody else took for granted, and he sometimes found him to be mildly embarrassing. They were passing a church one day when a wedding party was getting into

Chapter Five

black limousines to go to the reception. It was the custom for wedding guests to throw money—small change like pennies and ha'pennies and thruppenny bits—out of the car windows if any children happened to be present. Most children in the area knew when a wedding was going to take place, so one could count on their presence. If the guests failed to throw money, the children would shout, "Scabby wedding" at the departing limousines. So Jim and Ewan always welcomed the scene of a wedding and some extra change.

One day, Ewan announced to Jim, "Hey, look, a wedding."

"Where?" Jim turned around to watch black limousines approaching slowly along the street.

"You mean those cars?" asked Jim.

Ewan sensed something was wrong by the look on Jim's face.

"Honest to God, you're awfie stupid sometimes. Can you no tell the difference between a wedding and a funeral?" said Jim.

"A funeral? What's a funeral?"

"That's when somebody dies and they haftae take them tae the cemetery tae bury them and all the mourners go in the black cars. Don't people die in England and get buried?"

"Well, it looked like a wedding to me, although it wasn't outside a church, and it was going slower, I suppose. How can you tell the difference?"

"For a start, a wedding will have they big white ribbons on the front o' the car. That's one hint. Ach, it's a' right, ye'll learn aboot these things. I didnae think things were a' that different in England. Well, I'll tell you what, let's go up the Whin Hill and play for a while. It's a braw day, and it should be fun. Maybe Jim Berry's in at the farm at the bottom of the hill. If he's no, maybe Jim Barbour will be around up at the top o' the hill where his dad's farm is. If no, we can go catch minnows in the Beasy or fish for golf balls."

All these Jims, thought Ewan. *They must be short of names in Scotland.* Ewan welcomed the trip up the hill. It was Jim who introduced Ewan to the hills behind Greenock. Jim's father and mother and other family members delighted in visiting the wee tearoom at the place called the Corlic up in the hills.

A Different Place

The Corlic Hill had a big cairn at the top overlooking the River Clyde to the north. It was a stone's throw from the teahouse, which was really a wee barn next to the farmhouse in a wee valley surrounded by trees with a burn running next to it. A burn, Ewan was to find out, was a Scottish word for a stream or creek. It was a nice walk on Sunday afternoons—good fresh air and exercise.

It was Jim who showed Ewan the roads to Loch Thom, the Cut, and the old Roman roads and many other interesting spots in these hills. It was also Jim who seemed to know the names of every ship that sailed up and down the Clyde, where they were coming from, and where they were going. He knew all the tugboats and paddle steamers that plowed through the waves on their way to all the wee towns and villages on the Clyde coast and around the world. He could tell you which of Ritchie's ferries went where and at what times and where all the Clyde rowboat rentals were.

One of Ewan's favorite haunts was the top of the Whin Hill, which overlooked Greenock and was visible pretty well from any point in town. It wasn't far from Trafalgar Street. From there, he could walk past his school and a little farther to the outskirts of Greenock to the Berry's family farm, more commonly known as Berryards, and straight up the hill path to the top. It took maybe half an hour to reach the summit from Ewan's home, and the view was well worth it. Ewan took in the view mostly when he was alone. Ewan came to love these hills and would spend a lot of time on his own up there. Since his arrival from England, Ewan had to bear the brunt of a lot of teasing because of his English accent and different ways, and he used these hills as a way of escape. So it was there where he first met Winthrop of the Rockkin.

CHAPTER SIX

Grannie Kempock

GRANNIE KEMPOCK'S STONE stood on a precipice on Hillside Road overlooking the West Bay and Albert Road, which headed west out of the main part of the small town of Gourock, a wee resort town on the shores of the River Clyde right next to Greenock. Grannie Kempock's stone could talk or, more aptly put, could converse.

Every Sunday during the summer after the Coupars came to Scotland, weather permitting, Gran would take Ewan and Heather to Gourock to spend the day at the shore. There was no sand—only rocks, big and small. Gran's favorite rock was the one she called Grannie Kempock. She knew it wasn't really Grannie Kempock's stone, but it was her favorite stone to sit on at the shore while Ewan and Heather looked for seaweed and crabs and anything else they could discover in the ponds among the smaller rocks when the tide was out.

Grannie Kempock

Gran later explained her little fib because had she really wanted to see Grannie Kempock's stone, she would have to huff and puff up the hilly streets behind Gourock or climb a series of steep steps up a wee lane from Shore Street. The real stone stood all by itself, overlooking the Clyde. It was a big block of stone about the size of a man or woman, almost looking like a man or a woman, now circled by an iron fence. There were, of course, stories surrounding its existence. One story was that it was a witch turned into stone. Ewan didn't believe this; he sensed the stone had stood there long before the existence of witches.

Other theories were much more interesting and kept people coming to view the stone. Perhaps she was a sailor's wife who was watching for him to come sailing up the Clyde after a long sea journey but he never did return. She died up there and turned to stone while waiting for him.

Some people sketched her, and some took photos, but nobody stayed too long to keep her company.

Even Ewan was disappointed when he discovered where the real Grannie Kempock stone was. He didn't tarry long—until he found out that folks could talk to rocks.

It was a few months after their move to Greenock when Ewan learned of Grannie Coupar's stone and how she would talk to it, although it never talked back to her—or so Ewan thought. But there was a reason she always went to the same spot.

That's how it was that Ewan discovered this ability of talking to rocks and boulders. He had never heard the stones talking back until…well… this is the way it happened.

CHAPTER SEVEN

Meeting Winthrop

ONE FRIDAY AFTERNOON toward the end of his first year at school, after a day of teasing and a difficult math class, Ewan headed to the Whin Hill. He went straight up the narrow path from the upper end of the town to the top of the Whin Hill just before the golf course and the Beathe Dam. (The locals called it the Bease Dam or up the Beasy.) Here was Ewan's favourite spot: a big boulder that was almost designed to be sat on. He came to escape the constant teasing he endured about his English accent. Although he was beginning to fit in, he was still...different, and this was an escape from all of that.

Besides being a comfortable place to sit, the boulder had a magnificent view. On days with the sun shining and clouds across the sky or hanging over distant hills and the river flowing, the imagination could run wild.

Meeting Winthrop

With nobody but the sheep and rabbits for company and the other rocks and boulders among the coarse grass, whin, and gorse, Ewan could talk aloud to his rock seat. So he talked out loud with nobody to think he was going crazy. Talking out loud seemed to make his conversations with this rock seat seem more real. Apart from the occasional vacant stare from sheep, the rock seemed to give him some amazing answers.

"I wonder what all this looked like years ago," Ewan said.

"How far back are you thinking?" the rock seemed to ask.

"Well, how far back can you remember?" asked Ewan.

"For some period, I was surrounded by trees and couldn't see much but animals. They were not what you see now."

"Really?" Ewan said aloud. "What would you see?"

"Wildcats, fierce bears, wolves, and creatures now that you know of only in your Faerie tales and storybooks. And in the sky, when I had glimpses, there were many eagles and falcons. But before them there were indeed dragons. Before the dragons, I could not see much, for I was covered by earth and grass and other forms of vegetation, and the forests were thick. So even after I saw the light of the sun, I was every so often covered by leaves for many days until the strong winds blew over. And what winds we could have."

Ewan was intrigued by these observations. It was as if he would not have thought of some of these things himself and they were answers from the rock.

"What else do you remember?" Ewan asked aloud.

"Apart from early ancestors of your own and my own, I suppose, there were many other beings. I have been sat upon by Trolls and Goblins and have had wee folk and Faerie folk hide behind me."

"Here?" asked Ewan.

"Oh aye, many years ago now since they left, but there were many. The river brought too many other types, and the earlier ones didn't get along with them, so they found other places to go. Some of them still hide beneath these hills."

Many times, it seemed that the rock was indeed supplying the answers, but Ewan's dad always did say he had a good imagination.

Chapter Seven

Aloud, Ewan asked, "What about the river? Tell me about the river. What did it bring?"

"I do remember seeing large and fierce sea creatures, along with almost humanlike sea life, perhaps what you now call Merpeople or Selkie. I hear they retreated to the islands many miles north of here, where there are many more caves and more open waters for their protection, and where they can practice their powers, which you folk sometimes call magic. My family tells me these places are less accessible to your kind."

"Who tells you that?" asked Ewan.

"My family," said the rock. "We are many, and we pass intelligence and information many miles. We can sometimes change our rock being and be other things."

When thoughts like this crossed Ewan's mind, he wondered whether it was time to move on or go home. His rock seat seemed to indicate that rocks could visit one another; but it was his time and he did enjoy it, and he was never the worse for it. Sometimes he wondered if what the rock told him, he learned in books later or he heard it from his rock first.

"What happened when more people came?" Ewan wondered aloud.

"Ah well, that's when I was more able to see the changes. After I reached above the roots of the trees, I could see the trees cut down to use for building ships and houses. I had never seen those things, but my family passed images along. When I did finally view them, they were not what I could see in my own visions. Your kind looked strange, ugly and destructive to me, although I do remember I was once like you. Trees were murdered all around me and carried off. I see these boats and houses they were used to make and wondered of this existence. People had to move over land and sea to live in one spot. It was hard to understand, always moving to stay someplace."

Ewan spent many solitary moments on top of the Whin Hill this way, until the day he discovered he wasn't really alone with just the sheep, the rabbits, heather, and wind.

One day, after a thoughtful half hour with only a few questions, Ewan said aloud, "I wish you could really talk. I wonder if my thoughts are things that could really be true."

Some silent moments followed, and a voice seemed to say, "Your thoughts? What do you mean, 'your thoughts'?"

The rock, it seemed, really spoke this time.

"Ah, now you are thinking silently to me instead of talking aloud. I'm under the impression that all this time you haven't believed all that we've talked about. Do you think you have been dreaming? Well, I can talk aloud if you wish."

More silence, and Ewan slowly raised himself from his seat and retreated to a smaller rock. He stepped up to look at the place where he had been sitting. He was scared to ask the question.

"Speak again," he said.

"Well, well, well, and all this time I was under the impression that... well, I should say I'm almost speechless," said the rock.

"But how?" said Ewan.

"How?" asked the rock. "I thought your grandmother told you how. I see now that she hasn't and that you can't know that she talks to us. Her best friend rests on the shores of Gourock. Don't you know? But why didn't I realize this? You just came up here and randomly chose me to ramble on. Well, we have to talk now. Kind of like starting over. I suppose I should introduce myself, although we've known each other for many months. I'm Winthrop. Pleased to meet you. I am a Rockkin. I am a spirit of sorts. I was once like you until I was allowed into...we can get into that later."

"I'm...eh...I'm Ewan."

"I know who you are. Actually, I'm probably more surprised than you are at this."

"No, you're not," Ewan shot back.

"How about," said Ewan, "how about I come back tomorrow after I talk to my Gran? That will give me time to think."

The rock seemed disappointed. "We are still friends, aren't we? I hope this...er...little mix-up can be overlooked. Yes, talk to your Gran, but please return tomorrow."

Even the sheep seemed to be paying attention now.

"Do they know about what you are?" Ewan asked about the sheep.

"Well, yes. Who else do you think I talk to? Although," Winthrop said, lowering his voice to a thought, "they are not as entertaining as you, but they are not as stupid as people think they are."

Ewan looked at the sheep apologetically and smiled. "Tomorrow then," he told Winthrop. "Do you talk to others?"

"Oh, my friend Surston and...well...enough for now, until tomorrow then."

Ewan kind of waved at the rock Winthrop, then turned and left. In a few paces, he reached the path down the hill. He ran, jumped, and almost tumbled till he reached Berryard's Farm. What he didn't realize at the time was that he had not actually touched the ground for several feet but floated, one might say. Winthrop watched Ewan from the top of the hill, while another voice said, "He seems to have it strong, I would say."

"Yes, he does, Surston. Yes, he does."

On reaching the farm, Ewan broke into a steady run as if to escape the smell of the pigsties. He hopped over chickens and ducks until he was under the railway bridge and the upper end of Lynedoch Street and the sugar factories. He slowed down when he came in sight of some of the factory workers but steamed home down Trafalgar Street till he was close to the entrance of his tenement. He slowed down and then bounded up three flights of stairs to confront Gran.

"Gran...the rock," he said. "I mean Winthrop, it..."

Gran stopped him before going into the kitchen. "Dinna be in such a hurry." She quickly put her finger to her lips. "Whisht!" She then said aloud, "Your daddy's hame."

He caught his excitement in time, for he knew Dad wouldn't understand *this* stretch of imagination.

His father sensed something unusual but simply said, "Did you rip your pants again? Oh well, at least that's your play clothes you're wearing."

Gran winked at Ewan and later said, "Aye well, it seems we have to talk. I dinna realize you have the gift or I'd telt ye about it sooner. Say nothing to your father or grandpa. I'm fair excited nonetheless."

26

Meeting Winthrop

After dinner, Dad went off to the pub with some friends, for it was Friday night, and Grandpa went down to the Well Park for a game of checkers and some pipe smoking. Ewan's sisters were off playing somewhere. Gran was now ready for a wee chat. As much as Ewan wanted to know more, he was also eager to be off to the scouts meeting. That would be over by eight, and Grannie sensed that he might want to share this with his best friends.

"Don't talk about this the noo," she said. "You need to know more. And who of your friends would believe this, anyway?"

"But can I talk to your friend on the Gourock shore, Gran, and can we go on Sunday?"

"Aye, we could," said Gran, "but did you know that you can talk to any of them now if they want to talk back tae ye? And my friend at the shore is Victoria. She was called many names before that, but she liked Queen Victoria and always dreamed of being part of the Victoria Tower. But since that was impossible, she had her friends change her name to Victoria in 1892."

"I can talk to others?" Ewan asked.

"Aye, but you have to know how tae start up with them. Some in the past have started talking away just because some fool human was talking to himself. And in their world, that's unusual, so you can imagine what a body thought when he heard a rock or boulder talking back at him or her as the case was. So you see something had to be figured out. Although some stones have had fun with that by confusing many a poor soul wi' too much tae drink.

"Well, so you see there is some words to say or think that will be of help to start up a conversation, and they have their own language too, ye ken. Your great-uncles could talk to them too, ye ken. That's what took them into the mist. Well, part of the story goes. That's why it's still a sore point wi' your grandfather."

"Winthrop said they were part of another world or knew of another world, I think," said Ewan.

"Aye, that would be Diterra. There's the Realm of the Faerie Folk, and there's ours. Diterra is in between; it's a world in the mists," said Gran.

Chapter Seven

"But away tae the scouts wi' ye, and you'll learn more as time goes on, but keep it in your ain head the noo, laddie, promise me that."

"I will, Gran," Ewan said, and off he went to the scouts. He imagined all evening long that he could talk to buildings. But did sandstone and granite belong to the family of Rockkin, or if they didn't, were they part of another group of beings in Diterra? He wished he had asked Gran a word or thought to start something, but there was time for that instead of having a string of talk with strange buildings on the way to the church hall where the scouts were meeting.

CHAPTER EIGHT

Ewan and Winthrop

EWAN WAS UP early on Saturday morning. He cleaned out the fireplace, took the ashes to the midden, helped Gran with the food shopping, and waited for her to give him permission to head off to the Whin Hill to see Winthrop.

"Just you be careful now, son, and keep yir head and don't go bletherin' tae folk that wouldnae understand," said Gran.

"OK, Gran. I think I might meet Surston today. He's another Rockkin, I think, and I'm going tae ask Winthrop where they came from. They must be very old, and something else, Gran. You mentioned…um…about my great-uncles meeting them and about a mist or something. Should I know more?"

Chapter Eight

"I thought maybe you missed that, me and my big mouth, but I suppose at this point you should know. But don't talk aboot this tae yir grandpa. Ye'll understand why efter I tell ye. But no the noo, we need more time tae sit doon and chat awhile, so away ye go and meet Winthrop, and perhaps the morn we can go tae Gourock."

It was not long after Ewan was seated on the boulder when Winthrop made his presence known.

"Sleep well?"

"Aye, I did. What about you?"

"We don't really sleep, but we do rest. So what would you like to talk about today? I suppose that you're curious now about other things and not just what this place was like in the past."

"I still want to know more about that, but I want to know more about you now. And do I get to meet Surston? Gran's going to take me to Gourock on Sunday to meet Victoria and Grannie Kempock."

"Och, well, that will be a treat. Where do we start? Do you know much of the history of Scotland, especially about around here? It would help me explain things easier."

"Not really, I don't, except that there were lots of trees before and dragons and all those other creatures you told me about, unless you were putting me on."

"I would not do that at all, at all. Let me see…hundreds…well, actually thousands of years ago, this was a place of great forests, big trees of all kinds. There were oak trees the size that you couldn't imagine and all kinds of others like rowans and ash, alders and elders, and whitethorns. There were great boulders beneath them, and around them there were mushrooms and toadstools and lovely plants like harebells, primroses, pansies, thyme, ragwort, cowslips, clover, and bluebells. Och, and there were great bushes and…" Winthrop's voice seemed to be slowing down, and it sounded sad. He stopped for a bit, and Ewan said nothing. Then he started again.

"Everything was alive, you know, with all kinds of…spirit life and Faeries and other beings that would be difficult to describe to you. I was human like you, a young priest, a bit like your own minister, but we were

Druids. There was lots of learning to be done, and it was difficult to become a Druid priest or priestess, but it was worth it all. We learned to live in harmony, the humans, the Faeries, the animals, and the earth. The trees and plants would give up their leaves and petals to let the Faerie folk make healing potions, and we would plant the seeds into the earth to provide food. We would protect and honor the earth, water, and plants in return. We were what you might call pagans. You might have heard bad things about pagans, but in time you will make up your own mind. Everything and everybody helped one another. But, as humans will do, some became dissatisfied. They wanted more. More land or more power. I'm not sure, but just *more*. They turned some of the Faeries and animals against themselves and against us. There seemed to always be fighting and bickering. The Faerie folk would become angry with us and do mean things to us."

Ewan, who had remained silent without the need to have things explained to him better, spoke up.

"I hope you don't mind my butting in here, but what would you do to the Faeries to make them angry with you, and how did they retaliate?"

Winthrop realized that he had been more or less reminiscing.

"What did we do to them, you ask? We stopped paying as much attention to the things we should have been looking after. We destroyed too much plant life, muddied too much water, thought only of ourselves instead of considering the needs of the animals and other lives around us. I mean, there were a lot of bad people who were getting out of control. They would wander into Faerie places, looking for Faerie secrets and Faerie treasures, treating animals badly.

"Some of us knew that we had to take care of the bad humans ourselves. We needed to make things right. We had to respect the trees and plants, the rivers, and our neighbors, even the sun and the moon, the night and day, and the rain. We could not, however, stop some fighting between neighboring tribes and neighboring chiefs. We were not what you would call a united people, nor for that matter were the Faeries, but to get to your next question. How did they punish us? They had many ways they could punish us: steal children, steal cattle, bring bad weather, cast spells to bring us bad luck, and even worse. Some of the things they did to us were evil, but then again, so were some of our ways. I remember horse-like creatures, beautiful and sleek they were, always seemed to be around lochs and waterways and always wet to the touch with seaweed or water plants in their manes or tails. They would tempt men to ride on their backs but immediately galloped off beneath the water and the waves and devoured the riders—ate them, I believe. Many people went missing that way. Sometimes innocent folk would be lured into Faeries' portals for some reason or another, and there they would eat food and drink wines of the Faeries and think that they had been inside Faerie caves for only a short time only to find that they had been in there for many years and were forgotten about on the outside. Some just turned to dust on reentering their own worlds."

Winthrop stopped for a bit as if to think. Ewan once again said nothing. Winthrop started again.

"But there came a point when we knew our way was ending. Invaders were coming in and introducing or forcing their own ways and religions on us. We Druids, well some of us, decided on something different—a way to save ourselves. The oldest and wisest Druid among us was Myrdryd. He kept order for many years and held court a few miles from here beside a huge rock that is now referred to as the Clochoderick Stone, the Stone of the Druids, where his spirit now resides. It's close by what is now the wee village of Kilbarchan just over the hills yonder. But over time Myrdryd changed. I was very young, but I do recall he traveled to many distant places, and every time he returned, he was stranger than when he left—actually, 'mad' is a better word. He was born near yon castle rock on the Clyde yonder, and it became his retreat.

"Myrdryd had become a recluse, but he seemed to find some sanity while dealing with the Faeries on behalf of the other Druids. With the help and advice of the Faerie folk, we became spirit beings, part of the world of the Fae. It was a pact negotiated by our wisest leaders. Our spirits were removed from our bodies and embodied in rocks. The rocks were not already being used by other Faeries, and so we became the Rockkin, spirits of the rocks. You will understand more as you learn that many earthly things are embodied by...well, Faerie spirits.

"But Myrdryd...he just...well he..." Once again, Winthrop's thoughts wandered off.

Ewan spoke up. "Please, Winthrop, tell me more about Myrdryd."

"Well, yes. After his spirit was embodied to the rock, his mind could not comprehend the change in the beginning. He was made part of their race. They turned him to a spirit, the first of the Rockkin. He was and is now the Fae. His mother was a special person in their world but not of this world. She was of a world out there beyond ours, one of the sky people, one of the big Faeries. Yes, yes, I'm beginning to remember, but Surston can tell you more about Myrdryd."

Winthrop paused, as if to think, and then continued.

"I'm told it took a powerful lot of magic to help us get this way and a lot of arguing took place among the different Faerie groups before there was agreement, but we were important to them, and their friendship to us was an important link to their survival. We knew little of each other's worlds, I suppose, until we became part of theirs. But in joining together in this way, we understood them a little better, and they understood us a little better, and together we could battle the evil. We were needed to protect a special place, but only the older, wiser Druids were told the details. I'm still learning. In fact, I'm not even sure how old I am. We were placed in a state of spirit suspension, my fellow priests and priestesses, but we were able to communicate with one another and did so constantly. I was embodied in this rock for many years before I realized where I was and what I could do. We were to be held in this state until..."

"Until now, you mean? To do what?" prodded Ewan.

"To do what? I...I don't know. Surston was, still is, my tutor. He can answer your questions where I cannot. Perhaps you are part of the reason, but why would you be?" Winthrop seemed to be confused and was searching for answers, but Ewan kept his questions coming.

"Will I meet Surston and Myrdryd?"

"I somehow doubt that you will meet Myrdryd, but certainly you will meet Surston. They helped another tribe of people, helped to protect them. They were the Picts, and I suppose they still are. But I'm sure they were allowed into the world of the Fae also. Then again, I was told, if my memory serves me correctly, that they already were Pixies. Yes, that's it, small Faeries. There is something strange about that whole time. Mmmm."

Winthrop was more or less talking to himself and almost forgot that Ewan was hanging on his every word. He was jolted back from his own thoughts when Ewan said, "The Picts. I've heard of them, but I thought they disappeared a long time ago."

"Ah! So you do know something of the history around here. It will make it so much easier for me to help you understand."

Ewan didn't know but said nothing.

What Winthrop hadn't mentioned was that the big Faeries were not originally of this world and many had fought for centuries against one another before finding a somewhat peaceful existence on Earth. Some could not return for their Faerie ships. Starships were damaged beyond use, so returning to the stars was not an option. As a matter of fact, their worlds were no longer habitable. How would Ewan understand that when Winthrop himself could barely understand?

"Well, well, there'll be time enough for that. I think you'll enjoy this touch of the Fae, this second sight that you have. Surston tells me it is very strong in you. There is something special, says he."

"A touch of the Fae. Aye, Gran mentioned that. You've talked of me to Surston, then? What else did he say?"

"I think he would rather meet you himself and talk to you. It won't be long before he calls for you and the others…"

"What others? What do you mean others?"

"Oh, I was just thinking out of turn, nothing at all, nothing to tell. Well, now, you should be away home and have your dinner. And make sure you get to bed early tonight. You have another exciting day tomorrow. I'll no doubt be talking to you soon, and I have to meet Surston now."

With that, Ewan said his good-bye and went off down the hill whistling. He liked whistling and was good at it. He was beginning to become known as quite the bonnie whistler, especially by his neighbors. Up and down the stairs of the close where he lived, it would echo and sound grand. He was learning quite a few of the old Scotch songs from his Gran, and the hills seemed to like it too. They seemed to echo his whistling right back to him. The sheep would stop pulling at the grass to listen. Sometimes, Ewan felt that there was more than sheep listening, but he didn't know who or what. He often felt he was being asked or prompted to whistle. One tune in particular was called *Paul's Little Hen*. He learned it from Grandpa and would sing it in his head as he whistled the tune.

Paul's little hen flew away from the farmyard,
Ran down the hillside and into the dale.
Paul hurried after but down in the brambles,
There sat a fox with a great bushy tail.

Cluck, Cluck, Cluck,
Cried the poor little creature.
Cluck, Cluck, Cluck,
But she cried in vain.

Paul made a spring but could not save her.
"Now I shall never dare go home again."

I wonder why they like that one, thought Ewan, never questioning who *they* might be. He would realize soon that he wasn't like most of the other children but that there were others like him. Oh yes, there were.

CHAPTER NINE

The Real Grannie Kempock

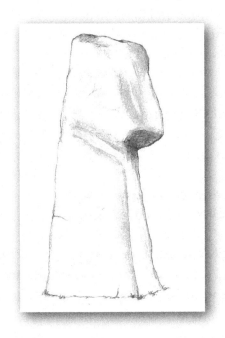

WHEN SUNDAY ROLLED around, the weather was sunny enough to warrant a visit to Gourock. Heather didn't want to go unless she could take a friend. This was usually not what Gran allowed. For her, this was a Sunday afternoon with her grandchildren and to visit her rock friend Victoria. Her eldest grandchild, Sally, five years older than Ewan, didn't fit into these Sunday visits. Ewan and Heather were two years apart, and if they could survive without arguing, it was pleasant for Gran. When they were alone together, they could accomplish this.

"But Gran, if you let Heather take Mildred to play with while you talk to Victoria, I can sneak up to see Grannie Kempock," Ewan said.

"I would like to see that," said Gran. "She will be surprised. I've no talked to her masel. But aye, it will be an experience for you to learn something, and I'll bet Grannie Kempock hasnae talked to anybody in years. Think the password for her and you can talk to her in thought in case there are other tourists around today."

"I will. I will be careful."

So it was that Gran settled down on Victoria, Heather and Mildred went off in search of crabs, and Ewan ran off to talk to Grannie Kempock in hopes of unraveling some mysteries about who she really was. A few people were coming and going, but no one was hanging around and nobody was saying anything complimentary except, "The view is nice from here."

"Why is there an iron fence around it?" someone asked. "It's not like we can pry that stone out and carry it off like a souvenir."

"No, not like the Stone of Destiny, the Stone of Scone," someone else added with a laugh.

Now there's a stone I'd like to talk to, Ewan thought.

"Perhaps if the fence wasn't there, someone would fall over yon wee cliff," a wee man said.

"Aye, some folk would be stupid enough, I can see," said his equally wee wife.

It was quite a few minutes before Ewan was entirely alone with Grannie Kempock, with nobody in view coming up or down the hill. Ewan just stood there and eventually thought one of the magic words. He got no response. He thought it again. He thought he heard a gasp or perhaps an exasperated sigh, then, "Who said that?"

"There's no one here but me," said Ewan. "I'm a friend of Winthrop's from the Whin Hill, and my name's Ewan. I'm standing right next to you."

"I can see that," said Grannie Kempock, "but goodness, nobody talks to me here. Who else do you know among us?"

"Well, my Gran is Victoria's friend down at the shore." Grannie Kempock seemed to make a sound of delight.

"Ah, yes. I talk to Victoria and she's told me of you and your Gran and sister. I've meant to pop down there some Sunday afternoon to meet you all, but I'm so busy up here at that time."

Ewan hoped she couldn't see a slight smile on his face as he looked around. "Oh," she said, "you just never know when you get busy. It's not like I talk to *anybody*, but I do like to be here when folks come around."

"Well, sure, I suppose. But I didn't know you could leave. I mean... well, how you do?"

"Oh," she said, "you *are* new. What do you know about us? I know your grandmother has been friends with Victoria for many years."

Ewan didn't know that. "But you, how long have you been part of us, so to speak?" asked Grannie Kempock.

"I have been talking to Winthrop for some time now, but I didn't really understand what was going on until two days ago." Ewan explained everything to her.

"My, my, my. I thought we had taken care of that problem a long time ago. I'm very cautious myself," she said. "I guess you are quite willing to learn more."

She waited for an answer. After a minute of silence, Ewan said, "I was going to ask how old you are and if you were once really a witch, and if not, how long have you been watching the river, and if you were a witch, who were you and..."

"Wait, laddie, wait laddie, hauld yer whisht. Slow down. I must say I'm flattered by all this interest." Ewan almost imagined a blush. "But if I told you anything, I would be less of a mystery, and I love being a mystery, and perhaps you might slip the truth out if I told you and diminish my entire mystique. Oooh," she wailed, "that would be terrible!"

Ewan thought there wasn't much difference between the male and female of the Rockkin and that of his own kind. Grannie Kempock seemed to have that feminine instinct of needing attention, just like his sisters.

"Well, who would believe me if I told them I talked to you? But then if anyone knew you talked, maybe you would get more visitors."

She thought for a few seconds. "Let's just wait and see how often you visit me now. Everything in time. Oh yes, and speaking of time, you should be getting back to Victoria and your Gran. I will let them know you're coming. Do come again. But before you leave, understand that I was never a witch but a Druid priestess, much like Winthrop and Surston."

Ewan waved as he left, as he had done with Winthrop. He wondered how they perceived folks and if they could see a wave. Winthrop had seen a lot, and this was something to ask either one of them the next time they talked. Or maybe Gran knew, since she had known them for a long time.

CHAPTER TEN

Avril the Witch

It was a few days after meeting Grannie Kempock when Avril approached Ewan in the school playground. Avril Maurton was one of his classmates. She had a dimpled smile, a smile that never seemed to fade, dazzling blue eyes, and long blond hair. She was smart without being overbearing. She always seemed to walk on her toes.

Along with Graham Austin, Ewan and Avril were as close as three children could be. Graham was almost the same size and weight as Ewan. He also had blue eyes and a winning smile—like Avril's in a way—with longish blond hair that he loved to let grow in front so he could chew it, which he did often in class as if to impress the rest of the students. Miss Weathers, their teacher, gave up asking Graham not to chew his hair, so it became a natural look for Graham as he sat at his desk. Oddly enough, his hair was combed back at other times. Graham, Ewan, and a tall, skinny boy named Hamish sat at the back right-hand corner of the classroom—spots reserved for the top students. The class was divided into two, with the girls to the teacher's left and the boys to the right. Avril sat in the top three in the girls' corner. Ewan and Graham often waited for Avril and walked her home together, a distance of maybe three-quarters of a mile, and each would part with her with a kiss on the cheek. If they didn't walk her home, it meant Graham and Ewan had football practice or something else after school. Rarely did one of them walk her home alone. They never thought about why, but it was a special bond. What they didn't know yet was the gift they shared.

"So," Avril said during a recess at school.

Ewan looked at her waiting for her to say something else.

"So," she said again.

"You said that before. It seems like you have something on your mind."

"Well, what do you think of your new gift?"

"What do you mean? Nobody gave me anything."

"Och, that's not what I mean."

"What do you mean?"

"You know, about your new friendship with Winthrop of the hill."

Ewan was stunned. He was about to say something when Avril said, "Och, it's OK. I know this must be confusing to you. You have what we call a touch of the Fae. It means you have a connection with the Faerie folk. There are lots of folk who have it but don't realize it. Some of them will never find out and live their whole lives without knowing it. If they never find it early enough, it fades. Others, like yourself, will stumble across it accidentally."

"How do you know about that? I mean, I never told you."

"That's because I have it too. I've known for a long while because my mother has it. She's a witch and also descended from the Faeries, you know, and so am I...sort of. I've recognized the gift in you for some time, but I didn't say anything because I usually wait for people to find out for themselves. There's more in our class you know who have it, but I'm not going to tell them."

Chapter Ten

It struck Ewan that his Gran had said something about others, and so had Winthrop.

"But why would you not tell them? I mean, shouldn't they know? I've known for some time I was a bit different, but I didn't know what it was. Like you say, a touch of the Fae. I told my Gran about it, and I think my Grandpa has it too, and I think my elder sister might even have it, but I'm still not sure what it is you mean. Can you tell me more?"

"Yes, I can. But not right now—perhaps after school. Graham has a dentist appointment so we can talk alone. Aye, I can help you find out more, but it takes quite a long while tae really find out just how you got it and how strong it is in you."

"What about the others? Wouldn't it be exciting to tell them?"

"Maybe, but it can be quite a powerful thing, and you have to know just how certain folks might use it," Avril said.

It suddenly occurred to Ewan that perhaps Graham also had the gift.

"Does Graham have it?" He knew by the look that Avril gave him that Graham did.

"Then we must tell him."

"I don't know. I wasn't even going tae tell you until you found out for yourself, but maybe he should know." Avril looked at the ground, and her long blond hair covered the expression on her face. "There are nine of us altogether, you know, but they're not all in our class. If we wait for some time so you can understand what this is like, then maybe we can decide which of the others should know. Maybe they'll find out for themselves without us telling them, just like you did."

"I've got a good idea," said Ewan. "Why don't we go and talk to Winthrop and see what he thinks. Have you met him?"

"No, I haven't, but my mother has. Well, not Winthrop exactly, but Surston. There once was a bit of friction between them, but I think that's in the past now. Yes, I think that would be a good idea. Winthrop knows a lot of the Faerie folk around here, and I would like to meet more of them."

"More Faerie folk? How many?"

"Oh boy! I'm not sure you know what you're in for, but let's find out," Avril said with a smile.

"Before you go, just tell me exactly: what is a witch? Because you don't really look like what I thought a witch should look like."

"I'm not sure you'll fully understand. When a Faerie folk marries a Landerfolk, that's a human who lives on earth, and they have children, and if the Faerie is the mother she would need a Landerfolk woman tae feed milk tae the baby. In that case, a Landerfolk mother who just had a baby and had milk would be stolen away to feed the Faerie baby. It wasn't always a nice thing to happen, but it did. While the Landerfolk mother is in Faerieland, she would be taught all kinds of Faerie magic, and then when she was no longer needed, she would be allowed to go back to her own kind. If she wanted to keep her Faerie powers, then she was usually turned into an ugly old hag, but some could bargain for a better outcome. One of my very distant ancestors was such a woman but before coming back was married to a male Faerie and had a baby of whom I am descended. I have considerable powers because of that."

A stunned Ewan said, "We should meet Winthrop."

Avril Meets Winthrop

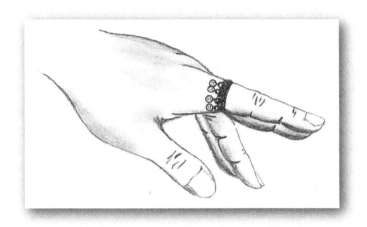

So it was decided. On a driech day that very weekend, Ewan would introduce Avril to Winthrop. He was a bit hard to find, perhaps because he wasn't expecting Ewan to show up with Avril, but appear he did.

"Well, goodness me," said a voice drifting through the breeze. "I never thought you could be such a picture of loveliness, Avril."

Avril blushed and turned away.

"Surston and your mother did not seem to get along for quite some time, and the way he described her and her daughter was never complimentary. But he can be a cranky old bugger and is not prone to giving compliments even when he does get to like somebody. You do look beautiful," said Winthrop.

"Speaking of looks," Ewan said to change the subject, "can you take on a shape other than a voice coming from a rock or stone?"

He wondered why he hadn't asked Winthrop this before, but his question was answered. A human shape appeared. It looked like it was made of grass and heather, or rather a translucent outline of a person. It also looked a bit like Ewan himself.

"We can do this. We can shape shift, as you would call it, and we can use many substances—even water. I can look like yourself, or if you can conjure up an image in your mind, I can do that too."

"Well," said Ewan, "I've thought of Surston as looking like a wizened old wizard, but I haven't thought what you look like. Do you have images of yourself?"

Winthrop said that whatever Ewan had in his own mind was what would appear. He said Rockkin could go into people's thoughts and pick out whomever or whatever they saw there. It had to do with telepathy—enabling conversations through thought. So Ewan tried a wizard lookalike. There he was, just like a wizard with a pointed hat, a wand, a flowing cape, and a stream of colours. Then he thought of Greyfriars Bobby, a Skye terrier famous for not leaving the grave of his owner, an old night watchman who was buried in Edinburgh's Greyfriars cemetery. The shapes melded while Ewan thought of different things but went back to the wizard. Then he had an idea.

"You told me that you were a person before you changed into this spirit form. Can you appear as you were as a human?"

"That's a good idea." Suddenly, a young man about six feet, four inches tall appeared in a brown tunic that came down to his knees and was tied at his waist with a rope. Around his shoulders was a brown cape. He had reddish-blond hair, thin on the top but floating to his shoulder blades, a rather large nose, and blue eyes. He was rather muscular. He seemed to tower over Ewan and Avril and appeared to almost float above the grass. Ewan had not envisioned Winthrop as such a giant of a man. The day was clearing, and the sun seemed to shine through Winthrop like glass. His brown cape at times took on a light shade of blue and floated as if caught by a breeze.

"Ah, I see I've startled you. Perhaps I should be…"

"Oh no, no, no. You just…well you…you look just how I thought you would look." Ewan laughed at himself as Avril playfully thumped the side of his head. "Can you walk with us also?"

Chapter Eleven

"Yes," Winthrop replied. "Let's go for a walk around the Beathe Dam and the golf course. It's been a long time since I've taken a walk."

Winthrop welcomed the company.

"I spend too much time with the sheep, been suspended in time for so long, but I believe I will start to move around a bit now. I want to see Victoria and Grannie Kempock."

"But what if I want to talk to you and you're not here?" Ewan asked with alarm.

"Just the power of thought will do. You'll see; it will work, just like it did when you and Avril got here. You thought of me and, in a way, called to me. And I heard you. Tell the truth, I like moving around. I wish I'd realized sooner that I was not so restricted after the Faeries changed me to spirit form. But then, until I met you, I had no reason to explore beyond these hills."

They stopped by the water at the dam. Ewan sat on a rock and talked to Winthrop as an image of his former self. A mist seemed to envelop them and move with them. It appeared suddenly and had a strange, captivating touch.

"What is this?" Ewan asked.

"Ah, this is a small part of Diterra, or the Land of the Mists. It is like a dimension between your world and the world of the Faeries, an in-between world. It protects them and allows them to remain unseen but at the same time be among Landerfolk and Landerfolk to be among them. It is like a portal to the real Faerie world. We wouldn't want those folk over there to see us now, would we?"

Ewan and Avril realized just how close they were to others and also a couple of dogs, but seemingly invisible to them.

"My Gran told me about this," said Ewan.

"Don't they see the mist, though, and can they not see into it?" asked Ewan.

Avril seemed to know the answer but let Winthrop go on.

"Och, I suppose they can maybe see a wee patch of mist, but is that not rather common up here?"

"So if we see mists, does that mean there's Faeries watching us or hiding from us?"

"You just never know now, do you?" Winthrop said with a wee twinkle in his eye. "What else would you like to know?"

"Actually…"

"I'm listening," said Winthrop.

"Well, it seems that most of my friends, like Avril here, know a lot more about Brownies and Selkie and dragons and stuff than I do, so I was wondering…"

"Go on."

"Well, are there Faeries everywhere, and what are Faeries exactly, and are there some I can meet right now? I mean friendly ones, of course."

"Oh aye. They are all around us. Some don't like to be contacted, of course, and some will not talk to you or make contact unless you invite them to."

Winthrop took on a serious tone and turned his attention fully to Ewan.

"You must learn this: there are Faeries of this world and others not of this world, the little Faeries and the big Faeries, *sidhe beg* and *sidhe mhor* in the Gaelic. I don't know if you will ever have a reason to meet the big ones, but you certainly can meet some of the Earth Faeries and spirits."

Winthrop turned to Avril. "You know this, I'm sure. Have you two not talked much yet?"

"I knew he had the gift, but I also knew he didn't know it himself until recently, and it's not like I've been in contact with the Faeries very much myself. Mum is quite protective, you know. She said some of the wee folk can be nasty and to take my time finding out about stuff. So I thought this would be a good way for Ewan and me to…well, meet and…you know, umm."

"Yes, quite right," said Winthrop. "And you are quite right also that there are some evil folk out there in the Realm of the Fae.

"I invite them then," Ewan said loudly, half expecting something or someone to appear almost immediately. He quickly added, "I mean the friendly ones."

"Hold on, hold on, not so fast," said Winthrop. "Some are ugly, at least ugly to you, but friendly. Their looks might scare you. That's why some are not always too keen to just go around introducing themselves. One of the friendliest, but scariest to humans, are the Urisks."

"Would you like to meet us?" This was a question not from Winthrop but from something or someone else. Ewan jumped and gasped. With hesitation, he looked at Winthrop.

"What can I expect?" he asked Winthrop.

"Talk to *us*, talk to *us*, talk to *us*," said a voice, this time sounding a bit like a mud puddle—bubbling, squelching, watery, and a little bit irritated.

"I will, I will, but tell me about yourself first, although you must be right around me somewhere," Ewan said.

"We love company, especially humans, and we won't eat you. Ha-ha, bubble, gurgle" said the Urisk. "Bad joke, bad joke. My name is Rankle."

"And I'm Woody," said another.

"How many of you are there then?" said Ewan, looking around.

"Well, are you ready? I think you are. We are highly intelligent, you know, just not pretty—to you. We think you are ready. Well, here goes." The mud seemed to rise up, brown and wrinkled, almost like foot-high frogs.

They took on odd human shapes with misshapen heads and an unusual combination of hair and feathers on their bodies. Their legs were stocky, and their arms stretched with hands clasped in front of brown wrinkly bellies looking somewhat like the bark of a tree. What clothes they may have been wearing seemed to meld with their brown wrinkly skin, hair, and feathers. The hair was curly and plentiful on top. Their eyes, though, looked strangely human and wise. Not just wise, but almost searching and merry. Without warning, the Urisks would have scared the bejeebers out of most people.

After a few moments of silence, Rankle said, "We thought the same thing when we met others not of our own kind. We think we are very handsome and our lady folk the same." With that, they rose to about three feet in height.

"We're not shape shifters, but we can adjust our size, as you can see," said Woody. "So here we are. While we're about it, we would like you to meet our friends, the Moor Pixies."

A wind seemed to stir a number of leaves, making a crinkling tingling sound as they were picked up by a breeze and brought forward to land a few feet in front of Ewan. Up rose a dozen or so of these leaves, which seemed to hover in front of Ewan before transforming into translucent Faerie bodies with fast fluttering wings turning golden as their bodies caught the rays of the sun. Almost at once, the grass and heather were covered in these Faeries. It was as if the rays of the sun had hit the water and were reflecting off everything else.

Rankle looked on before saying to Ewan, "Hold out your hand and introduce yourself, and tell them you wish to be friends. Sometimes it's the only way to do it. Humans have to make the first move. It has to do with making them know you believe in them, and then it's all right. They are as friendly as we are—much more magic, though."

Winthrop seemed almost as fascinated as Ewan and Avril as they watched this spectacle. He held out an arm as Ewan did, and a few landed on them like large butterflies. Woody said they were also called Heather Pixies.

"We are so pleased to meet you, Ewan and Avril, of course."

Voices were ringing as they hovered around, changing in size from six inches to three feet and landing on top of the heather without seeming to sink into it.

"How do you talk to them?" asked Ewan. "They keep moving and flying around and changing size."

"They're very excited," said Rankle. "They will settle down soon."

As if by a word, about two dozen three-foot-high Pixies seemingly stood on the tips of the grass.

One came forward. "It's been quite some time since we've had a gathering such as this, especially with Landerfolk, and you too, Winthrop. You'll forgive us, Winthrop; humans are so helpless when you consider what powers others in this world have. Have you told Ewan and Avril what magic the Faerie folk have?"

Ewan seemed alarmed. He looked around and saw other Urisks. They appeared to be enjoying the company as a rare occasion indeed.

"Oh, Ewan's not quite ready to learn too much at once, but there will be time," said Winthrop.

Chapter Eleven

"Excuse me," said Avril, "but do you have names? Maybe not all at once," she added after noticing the numbers.

"Of course," said a Pixie. Ewan couldn't tell if they were male or female. When a few names were offered, they didn't help. Maybe Avril knew.

"We, like Winthrop, use names of the land around us."

It suddenly occurred to Ewan that Winthrop's name came from the Whin Hill.

"Well, I am Beathe," said a Pixie who appeared to be the spokesperson for the group. *Oh, there was an island in the small loch called Beathe Dam,* Ewan thought.

Beathe continued, "This is Goff, and this is Isla."

The Pixies all looked the same. A thought flashed through Ewan's mind telling him in time he would be able to tell them apart. He wondered from which new friend this thought had come and wished he was psychic. *You are. You just haven't used it yet.* Goff smiled, and Woody gave him a thumbs-up.

A sudden mist seemed to catch everyone off guard. It was unlike what they were already experiencing and appeared almost like a flash with many colours and shapes. It seemed to freeze everything it surrounded, but then a warm sense of friendliness took over. Suddenly, many figures mounted on white horses were everywhere. Bells hung from the reins of the horses and chimed many notes, but no saddles were on these mounts. Colours of the rainbows seemed to be reflecting everywhere, and a collective chorus seemed to utter the name Aubrey several times. Though taken aback, Winthrop stepped forward.

"My my. This is an unexpected pleasure." He seemed to hesitate before turning to Avril and Ewan.

"This, my friends, is Aubrey, ruler of the Elves, and these are...Elves."

Aubrey turned to look at the children. *She is the most beautiful girl I have ever laid eyes on,* Ewan thought. He saw a girl with long brown silken hair, eyes that seemed to be made from pools of water...

Before he could gather his wits, Avril's thoughts took over. *Aubrey is the most handsome man I've ever seen.*

She saw a tall muscular youth with bare marble white arms and dark hair flowing over his shoulders. Both of them saw long pointed ears and eyes that were not round but oval. It wasn't long before Winthrop broke the spell.

"As I said, this is Aubrey, and Aubrey appears as Aubrey wishes to." Then, turning to Aubrey, he said, "This is…well…what can I say but the obvious, very surprising. Why have you come?"

Aubrey slid from the horse and approached the party.

"The Seelie Court wished me to meet them and…" Before Aubrey could say more, Winthrop gasped.

"The Seelie Court? But why?"

"Time will reveal why, but I have a gift for the children and their friends, whom I see are not all here."

Aubrey's voice sounded like something out of a song, with bells softly ringing every word. Ewan and Avril were enchanted.

"Take these rings; wear them as you wish. Others of the Faerie blood or the Faerie faith will see them, and they may afford protection in some ways. But be aware: in some instances, the reverse may be true. Use good judgment. If others are not able to see the rings, then they are not of the Fae."

Ewan and Avril turned their attention to the rings, which were black with several dangling two-linked chains. On the end of each link was a small red stone. Ewan and Avril put on the rings, which seemed to fit perfectly. But they felt no different.

"Winthrop will have more in his possession when they will be ready to give out. We must leave you now, but we will have many occasions to meet again."

And quite as suddenly as they arrived, they departed. A huge colourful mist appeared, and an army of horses and Elves rode off. The atmosphere was electric—silence first, then a slow murmuring of excited chatter. Winthrop looked amused and bewildered at once.

"Who are the Seelie Court, and why haven't we met Surston yet?" Ewan said.

"He was with us, but too much was going on, so he let me know that another time would be better to meet you both," said Winthrop. "And perhaps some of the others too."

Chapter Eleven

"You know of the others? Of course you do. That's what you meant when you said...But the Seelie Court, who are they?"

"They are the big Faeries who are from another place, and the little Faeries who are from here. Some of them you've just met. I will let Surston explain more about them."

Ewan's thoughts were racing on the way home through Berryard's Farm down to the streets, and he realized that he and Avril had exchanged all kinds of thoughts all the way down—about the ugliness and friendliness of the Urisks, about how many other Faerie types there were, and about what powers they had. There were so many different others, good Faeries, bad Faeries, Brownies, Wag-by-the-Ways Selkie, Pixies, Merfolk, Drakes, and Dragons, and the Seelie Court, whoever or whatever they were.

Back in the hills, Surston appeared to Winthrop looking concerned. Winthrop waited for Surston to speak.

"The children are in danger, or Aubrey would not have appeared at the request of the Seelie Court. Something is amiss. I felt from the start of all this that it was a strange occurrence for all these children to be coming together at once. We must find out what it is. I think that because the young ones still believe in the Faeries, the Faeries trust them. You remember Mr. Barry's story about Peter Pan: if you stated that you didn't believe in Faeries then a Faerie would die. What really happens, as you know, Winthrop, is that if a person says something like that, that person is really stating his disbelief in the Realm of the Fae, and it is that person who is dead to the Faeries. All too many Landerfolk are taught early that Faeries are nonsense. What a shame," he said with a sigh.

"The children will no doubt be unaware at this point that a number of the Fae folk are not as friendly as those they have just met and many dangers lurk. Dark forces from the east are getting too close to the secrets that the Fae have been guarding for centuries. We must communicate with the Picts and, if possible, the Seelie Court, to find out what they may or may not know, and we must be kept up to date for the sake of the children. I feel that there are more than just bad Faeries they have to look out for."

"But what if you are wrong?" asked Winthrop.

"You know I am not. The minister…I have to talk to the minister very soon."

"What minister?"

"You know very well what minister. I mean the one who was attacked in the hills recently. It's not common knowledge yet, but I fear it will be. He will be talked of as a loony, but you and I know better."

CHAPTER TWELVE

The Others

"WE HAVE TO tell the others about their...um...gifts, Avril. We just have to. This could be so much fun for all of us," said Ewan.

"I think you're right, but we still have to be careful," Avril said.

"Well, who are they?"

"I will tell you now if you promise not to go blurting this out to them before making some sort of a plan. I mean, you don't just go up to somebody and say, 'Guess what? I know something about you that you don't know,' and then just blether it out. They'll think you're daft tae start with. Besides, I'm not entirely sure, some of them might know already."

"But I thought you could tell," Ewan said.

"Some I can, but there are a few of the others who...well, they just might have the ability to hide it, which would actually be a wise thing to do. Something you might want to think about," said Avril. "I will show you how to do that. Don't want you getting yourself intae…well, some kind of trouble."

"Now you're scaring me."

"Well, just think about it. I'm not trying to scare you, but lots of people don't believe in Faeries, and they might think we're daft."

"OK. You can trust me to do it your way. I mean, you're the witch, and I wouldn't want to get you mad at me," Ewan said with a laugh. "So, go on. Tell me who the others are."

"Well, there's Graham. You know that already, but he doesn't…yet. There's Leslie, and I know he doesn't know."

"Leslie…you mean Leslie around the corner from me?"

Around the corner from Ewan's tenement building, on Roxburgh Street, lived Leslie MacCaum. Leslie was a good six inches taller than Ewan and Graham and had short reddish-blond hair. He was a few pounds heavier, though not fat, but he fit right into the circle of friends. He was a football fanatic and passionate supporter of the Glasgow Rangers, not the local Greenock Morton. For some reason, Ewan and his sister were assigned to a different school from the one the others in the immediate neighborhood attended, so it was that Ewan developed circles of friends who included neighborhood and school pals.

"Yes," said Avril, "and don't keep interrupting every time till I've finished. Then you can ask questions. There's your cousin Brian."

"Brian? My cousin Brian?"

"Yes, and stop interrupting me. Billy Milaun, Shauna McPhail, Pauline Marshal, that English girl, and Belle Aunders are the others. There are nine of us altogether."

Everybody liked Ewan's cousin Brian Coupar, with his crazy tricks and jokes, but on his serious side he loved to fish. He was similar in stature to Ewan and Graham, as was Billy, but Billy had an unusually round face and big ears that made him easy to spot in a crowd.

The girls were as different as could be, but they had one thing in common: they were all unusually pretty. Shauna was tall for a girl. She had short dirty-blond hair cut bluntly just below her ears, pageboy style. Belle was of average height with green eyes and light-brownish hair, almost to her waist, that she loved to toss around. Pauline was an English lass living in Scotland with equally long hair but dark and silky. Her English accent seemed to be more captivating than Ewan's. *Just 'cause she's a girl*, Ewan thought.

"But my Gran and Grandpa are touched with it too, and so is my elder sister," said Ewan. "Maybe my younger sister and my cousin Jim have it."

"I know that. So do my mother and lots of folk I don't know, I'm sure. But I thought we were going to have a wee group here, like a secret group so we could explore and have fun with this," Avril said. "I'll tell you one thing: I hope your cousin Jim doesn't have it. Although he's all right, sometimes he can be dangerous. If he does have it and doesn't know it, I'll never tell him. And Heather...well, if she does have it, I'm sure she'll find out herself."

"Oh aye, I see what you mean, but should we not let anybody else know who's in our circle of friends?"

"I think if we're going tae have a wee secret group, that's just what it should be. People are funny, ye know. We might all get burned as witches if anybody finds out," Avril said with a laugh. "Promise."

"Aye, I promise," said Ewan. "When do we let the rest know? Oh, what about the rings? We could wear our rings, and if they see them, it would mean...well...if they didn't know about the rings...well."

"Let me think on it," said Avril. With that, both went home with lots on their minds.

CHAPTER THIRTEEN

The Nine Come Together

After some thought, Avril came to the conclusion that it would do no harm to let all nine know. Although Avril's closest and most trusted friends were Ewan and Graham, Leslie, Brian, and Billy were the closest others she could think of to trust. It was funny that they should be the ones that Avril had identified as having a touch of the Fae.

It seems that the connections and beliefs of some of the older folk were still strong and had been passed down to the next generation without their knowing. Some of the Faerie folk were not shy about showing themselves to Landerfolk with connections that went back many years, maybe centuries. This, in a way, made it easier for Avril to concoct a plan to enlighten them all. Avril said nothing for a week about the meeting with Winthrop and the Faeries, and Ewan seemed content to wait till she mentioned it again. So it came as a surprise to Ewan when she suddenly let it drop on Graham. The boys were walking her home when she suddenly changed the subject from homework to magic.

"Do you believe in magic and Faeries and things like that?" she asked Graham.

A puzzled look crossed his face, but he smiled and said, "Not really."

"What do you mean, 'Not really'?" Avril shot back.

"Well, who knows for certain when you hear all those Faerie tales? Some of it sounds like it could have been true a long time ago."

"Well, we know for certain, Ewan and I. Don't we?" She turned to look at Ewan, who stared back dumbfounded. Looking back at Graham, she asked, "Do you know what a touch of the Fae is?"

"Aye, I've heard of that—the second sight or something."

"Well, you have it. So does Ewan. He knows he has it now. And until this moment, you didn't know, but now you do."

Ewan had absolutely nothing to add as Graham turned to look at him. "What is she on about, and what does this have to do with homework?"

"What she means is that…" He turned to Avril and said, "I didn't think you were just going to tell him like this."

"This was Shauna's idea, and Pauline and Belle agreed. You see, I found myself in their company earlier this week, and I just happened to say something about you two. Pauline asked if I had put a spell on you 'cause you're always with me. I asked them what they meant by that, and Belle said, 'Oh, we know you're a witch, and we were wondering if we could all be friends because you know about us.' We all laughed at the whole situation and finally got to talking about Graham, Leslie, Billy, and Brian, and Shauna said just tell them. So I just did. Belle is going to tell Brian, although she thinks he knows, and Pauline will tell Billy, and we thought you should let Leslie in on it."

"I still don't know what you're talking about," said Graham. "I've heard of the Fae, but I don't know what it is. And what dae ye mean you're a witch?"

"I am a witch," said Avril. "I was born a witch. My mother's a witch."

Graham's mouth was open. "Noooo…Really? I knew it!"

"What do you mean, you knew it?" Avril asked.

"I don't know what I meant. I...well...I just knew there was something different about you, in a good way, of course. I mean, you're just too pretty and intelligent." He had never said these things to her before. "That's not what I meant either," he stuttered. "What I mean is, you are actually one of them, and we didn't know it? We would never have known it if..."

He paused then said, "Are you trying to tell me that there are real Faeries and you know magic and...OK, what's the Fae?"

"Let's go tae the Well Park. It's early yet, and we'll explain it to you," Avril said. An hour later, Graham sat beaming at the thought of it all.

"So, what happens now? Dae I get to know real Faeries, and dae I get to do magic and stuff?"

"Ye know what I think would be good? After you tell Leslie, and I think you should tell him soon, we should all get together and form a wee club like Ewan and I talked about and swear tae secrecy and see where it takes us from there. Leslie's the last one, and I think you should just let him know the way the others found out, like Graham did."

Avril sat back on the park bench, smiled, and raised her eyebrows. "Well, Leslie's next."

CHAPTER FOURTEEN

The Cruach Is Formed

"So, Leslie, we're having a wee picnic this weekend. Are you coming?" asked Avril.

"Of course, but you don't really think I believe all that stuff, do you?"

"Ah, well, I see Ewan and Graham did talk to you then. That's good. What fun we're going to have. Your folks are from Ireland, are they not?" Avril didn't wait for an answer. "I've been doing a wee bit of searching and found out that perhaps where one's family comes from might have a bearing on what Faerie connections a person might have."

"Oooh, so you might expect me tae bring a Leprechaun or something, is that it?" joked Leslie. "I'll see what I can do."

"Don't bother just now," Avril said with a laugh. "You'll be meeting enough of the others this weekend."

The Cruach Is Formed

The chosen spot was perfect. It was a mile or so past the dam on the way to the Corlic Hill. From the road to Loch Thom, an old Roman road veered to the left to Whitelees Moor, and a little farther on was a good view of the old Roman fort on Lurg Moor. The Romans had occupied this part of Scotland centuries ago, and quite a bit of evidence of them remained, but it was more than that. The moors up there had portals to all kinds of Faerie secrets that the group did not know about, but the boys had been drawn to it—for it was a good camping area. The hills were filled with Faerie cairns, and the teahouse in the wee farm below was in the middle of them. The Corlic Hill was a high point in the area and attracted many visitors. Ewan discovered this spot when traveling with cousin Jim and his aunts and uncles to the teahouse.

The nine of them were all together at last. They had brought sandwiches, apples, oranges, bottles of Barr's Irn Bru, and one or two other bottles of soda. They all planned a good long day, and nobody was taking it lightly as Ewan and Avril feared they might. There were still some doubters, but it was certain they wanted to believe.

They were lucky to have a perfect day for a picnic. Greenock was known more for its rain than its abundance of sunshine. It was said that the name Greenock came from an old Gaelic word *Grainaig*, meaning sunny side of the hill. Others said it was named after the large green oak trees that once stood in abundance around Scotland—especially Greenock—and one in particular that grew close to the river gave the town its name: the village of the Gren Ok.

After an hour of resting from the climb, it was time to focus on the group's reason for being there.

Avril started. "You know a little something about yourselves now. And I can sense certain auras when people have the gift. What I would like to point out is we are all one of them, as Graham put it. But some of your connections are weak and have to be developed. You must learn how to use them. That's why I picked you all."

"You picked us?" said Belle, "How?"

"Well, I didn't mean 'pick you.' I meant I picked you as friends because I could sense the Fae in you. You may not have realized it, but you probably felt it too; you just didn't know it at the time."

Chapter Fourteen

"So are we really goin' tae meet some Faeries or something?" Graham asked.

For some reason, everybody turned to Ewan. As he looked back at them, he was aware of a slight mist developing. He looked at Avril. It could mean only one thing.

"Of course we are, but it seems they're not quite ready to come forward." Ewan knew, as did Avril, that Winthrop was nearby wondering just how to make an entrance without startling some of them. "So I thought that maybe we'll tell you about some of them first."

"In the old times, people used tae see them a' the time," said Billy. "So why don't we now—especially since we're supposed tae have the touch?"

"Oh, but we do," said Pauline. "They are a bit more cautious these days, but I see them all the time. So does Shauna and now Ewan and Avril. Although I don't know why you haven't seen them or made contact with them before this." She looked at Avril.

"My mother is quite protective of me," said Avril, "because some of the Faerie folk don't trust or like witches or Landerfolk due to some bad experiences. You see, witches are still thought of as Landerfolk but with certain powers of magic, and some in the past have used it for evil. But we are not Landerfolk. There was a sorcerer who lived nearby here many years ago in a place called the Devil's Glen, the Glen of the Evil One. It's not far from here, but now they call it Dervol's Glen. They say some of his black magic is still felt at times around the glen. He was of the Fae and did a lot of harm tae Landerfolk as his way tae protect Faeries."

"Aye, it's not like some of those Faerie folk themselves are nasty beings," said Shauna.

Avril went on. "So although my mother and I are what we call white witches, we are still looked upon with some suspicion. I am not entirely a witch because one of my distant grandsires from the past, the very distant past, I might add, was an elf. I will tell you all more eventually, but I would like to hear all your stories."

Graham turned to Pauline and Shauna and said, "So tell us about the Faeries you've seen."

"We didn't just see them; we grew up with them," said Pauline. "Not together, of course, 'cause I just met Shauna about a year ago. But some have attached themselves tae families, almost like family members." She paused. "We have a Wag-by-the-Way."

Pauline explained why Wag-by-the-Ways were not seen as frequently. They loved fireplaces because they were often cold. They guarded homes, castles, highways, and byways in the lowland and border counties for certain families to whom they were loyal. They are small dwarf Faeries with long catlike tails and have spent so much time around the fireplaces that they have looks of cinder piles. Pauline's family called them collectively Wag-by-the-Way. One came north with Pauline's family when they moved from England. The days of guarding castles and homes are gone, and not many marauding travelers roamed the countryside any longer. The days of angry tail wagging were limited, although the Wag-by-the-Way still got angry when it sensed tinkers because it can't tell very well the difference between tinkers and Gypsies.

"Besides, lots of people are changing to gas fires now," Pauline said in her cute English accent. "And what Flamish liked best of all was those huge log fires in large fireplaces where the whole family could sit in."

"So Flamish is his name?" asked Leslie.

"Yes, we still have him because we live now in a cottage with a fairly large fireplace still in use. He spends some time with FireForge now, both being lovers of fire."

"Who is FireForge?" Belle asked.

Shauna chimed in. "I bet he's a Dragon who breathes fire."

"Well, yes," said Pauline. "I wasn't sure I should tell you. Some people are scared of Fire Dragons."

"What other kind is there?" queried Brian, echoing Ewan's thoughts.

"Well, there are the Vilebheist or Draygans, to use an easier term. They're a bit like fire dragons. But because they live in water, the fire's gone out, I guess," said Billy.

"How do you know about them?" asked Ewan.

"My family comes from Carbost, up in the Isle of Skye, and I used to see them in the waters around there along with the seals and well…

mermaids, I think, before we moved here. Haven't seen them for some time, though."

"Are they like Nessie?" asked Belle.

"Och no, and Nessie's real name is Urkhart. He's the one spotted most of the time, but they've gotten his gender wrong. But they're not the same. FlipFloggle is the Draygan. Looks more like a fire dragon than Urkhart does, but they cannae fly anymore. I think they used tae. You'll see them on the east coast aroon Aberdeen, 'cause they came, at least some of them, from places like Norway. They came here donkeys' ages ago, and they like the islands aroon the north from Orkney, Shetland, and the Hebrides on the west coast. They like a' the inlets tae go ducking in and out. Some have twa heids, so it looks like there are more of them than there really are."

"Aye, and they used tae give Selkie a rare auld time of it," said Shauna. "That was before they had tae learn to get along. Not that I remember, just what I remember being telt."

Shauna was born in Greenock, but her family was from Thurso, way up in the north of Scotland.

"So now you're going to tell us you're part Selkie?" said Ewan.

"No, no' that," Shauna said with a smile.

"But if you're not a Selkie, then what are you? Or what do you know of the other kinds of Faeries then?"

"We had Brownies," Shauna said after thinking a wee bit.

"Brownies," Ewan said. "What would Brownies..."

"Oh, I didnae mean what you're thinking of. I mean Faerie folk—that kind of Brownie, not the ones that are connected tae the Girl Guides. Don't get them mixed up wi' Pixies or Hobgoblins and things. There's so many of them, all quite different, really, although come to think of it, maybe not. Brownies are partly related to Leprechauns, so I'm told, although they're not quite as rich and flashy. They do like music and a wee nip now and again. They mostly stay out of sight, do house chores, sew, knit, spin, weave, cook, and all that. They like to be fed and supplied only with good milk and cream and things like that. They don't like rewards or special treatment, or they'll feel insulted and disappear and not come back tae a house that treats them like that. They make shoes, I'm told. Grannie had some at her cottage in Thurso, you know. Put the food and drink out every night, always gone in the morning."

"Well," said Ewan, "maybe she did it just to amuse you."

"You don't know my Grannie. She had other ways tae amuse bairns. The Brownies she takes seriously. Brownies weren't that common, but we had a few. It's awful cold and windy up there, and I was told it was the sea that had the most life. There weren't that many trees, so we didn't have the population of Wood Elves. That's tree spirits and tree Faeries that other areas have, but that meant we didn't have tae worry about the Ghillie Dhu either. Nasty things, they are. Don't like humans at all. Wrap you up in long green arms and make you slaves of the forest. When forests were cut down, a lot of human folk were set free after years of being enchanted by forest folk. Poor folk, wandering around years after their ain folk were dead and buried, trying to fit in somewhere. The Brownies helped a lot of them, you know. It was just that folk who had lived with these things in the hills and glens, along the coasts and in small villages, before moving to bigger towns and cities were quite used to this. By not mentioning much of it to city dwellers, they protected these so-called mythic folk. Life went on changing when it had to, but the magic never weakened. Back to the Selkies: sometimes the folk up there had to be warned when the Selkie were looking for poor women to trick into marrying. More often than not, we were warned in time tae trick them instead by finding their skins. They couldnae go back into the water without them ye ken. Sometimes it was the female Selkie who stole the menfolk." Shauna looked around at the group and nodded once.

"And this we should all take seriously too," said Avril. "Are we all in agreement? I mean, after all, this could be a lot of fun but serious stuff when you think about it."

"Aye, I suppose," Brian said. "But where do we go from here?"

"We form a wee secret society, the nine of us, and give ourselves a name. We tell Winthrop, Surston, and the faerie folk, and then...well, let's see where it takes us. I tried to think of a wee Gaelic name that would mean secret circle or secret circle of friends, but that was difficult. So I just made up a name." Avril looked around at the others. "It's Cruach, and to us it just means 'Circle of Friends.'"

There was silence until she added, "I know some of us are still a wee bit skeptical, but...what do you think, Cruach?" She looked around at them. As if by some hidden sign, they all said "Cruach" together.

"Oh, that was canny," said Shauna.

"It was, and suddenly I feel different since we all said that," added Belle.

They all nodded.

Ewan said, "Well, leave it up to Avril and me, and we will get together with Winthrop and Surston and let them know. I think maybe...well, they will still want to meet us all together. Anyway, let's get stuck intae they sandwiches and Irn Bru and have some fun while the sun is still out."

"Yer sounding more Scottish every day. There's hope fur ye yet, cousin," said Brian.

"Aye, but there's Pauline to work on next. She still sounds pretty English to me," Ewan said.

"Och, I think it's nice with her. She suits it more than it suits you. Besides, she was born in England. She's got an excuse, and you don't," said Billy.

So the Cruach was formed. Everybody was excited, happy, and ready for adventure.

"I just thought of something," Billy said. "What if we meet bad Faeries who want to hurt us?"

"Why would they want to hurt us, Billy? What do you mean?" asked Pauline.

"I've heard Faerie stories that are not all nice and well. What if we meet nasty ones?"

"He's right," said Avril. "And I did kind of think that. Well, something could happen if we're not careful. I did mention that to you, Ewan, if you remember. My mother knows that all too well. I think I have a plan."

"What plan do you have?" asked Billy.

The Cruach Is Formed

"You might have missed this from the past couple of days, but maybe some of you saw this in the *Telegraph*. I know Ewan did, about the hikers who were attacked."

Ewan remembered sitting in the kitchen when his Grandpa was sifting through the evening paper.

News: Hikers Attacked

"Oh my, look at this! Almost missed it," Grandpa said as he shook the paper and folded it so Gran could read the small column on the front page. "Hikers attacked on Ben Lomond."

The article explained how a group of hikers, three men and two women, were attacked out of the mist by what they described as a beast with a big spiky club, one big arm, and a big eye in the middle of his head and hopping around as if he had just one leg. They had gotten lost in the mist and, following advice of hiking associations, remained for a couple of hours in one spot. Wandering around the mists, a hiker could end up walking off the edge of a cliff or steep path and getting hurt. Some mists didn't last long, while others could last for days, but it was always best to stay put if you were not familiar with the area. These hikers tried a bit of yelling.

"And would ye look at this—one of yon hikers was Mr. Gillanders, the minister from the kirk you go to. I ken he's taking a wee break, but to go hiking? That's what probably caught the attention of the Fachan," Grandpa said.

"Och, away and not be talking about these things in front of the boy. It disnae say it was a Fachan," said Gran.

"It describes a Fachan," said Grandpa. "And besides, the boy's no' that unaware of these things, I've noticed recently."

"What's a Fachan, Grandpa?" said Ewan, flashing a look at Gran. "You know, she's right. I'd like to know more."

"Well, a Fachan is a nasty beastie of a man who lives on the mountaintops in the Hielands. Just in the Scottish Hielands, ye ken. There's one for every mountaintop, and there's something about defending the mountaintops. Just what's up there to defend, I don't know. That is anybody's guess. They don't like anybody or anything, including one another."

"I heard there is only one, and he's called Peg Leg Jack," said Gran.

"He seems to get from one mountaintop to another awfie quickly, then," said Grandpa. "Besides, my ain Grannie aye said there was more than one. She was from the Hielands, you know."

Grandpa looked at Ewan. "Dinna forget that, yir Great-Grannie's frae the Hielands."

Ewan nodded his head, and Grandpa went on. "Nothing like that's been seen for years. In fact, I've never seen them, or it, if ye want, mentioned in any modern newspaper. Just the auld folks mention things like that noo and again."

"Aye, and it's been a few years too, even before your Grannie's time that it's been seen," Gran said.

"Why would it all of a sudden appear now?" asked Ewan.

A long silence followed. Ewan changed glances from Grannie to Grandpa.

"Well," Grandpa said as he reached into his jacket pocket for his pipe and tobacco, "that's a good question."

It looked like he was thinking up a good story while he cut his tobacco, shredded it in his hands, put it into his pipe, and lit it, whereupon he would slip off his bonnet, polish his bald head, put his bonnet back on, take the pipe out of his mouth, and settle into his tale. It usually was a good one, and nobody minded waiting.

Chapter Fifteen

"You know, it's said that the Fachan had less reason for chasing away strangers since less Hieland men and women live there these days. So he went inside the mountains tae bide his time." With a quick look at Gran, Grandpa whispered to Ewan, "I'm saying him alone for noo, but I still think he's no alone up there."

Grandpa was thinking. He wasn't focused on the story now, but letting his mind wander trying to figure out the truth of it all. "There's more than just him lives in yon mountains and caves."

It was like he was not just talking to Ewan and Gran but trying to reason out something. "I'm no just talking about the close-tae-the-sur-face folk, but away doon inside, there's them that's no been seen for years. Savage fighting wee men wi' red hair and lovely goddess women folk. It was always said that sometimes they ventured oot tae prowl around, and auld Peg Leg and his cronies cleared the way every noo and again."

"Ach, there was more whisky talk in yon auld tales than not," Gran said with a wave of her arm.

"Well, sometimes it took a wee dram or two tae get the stories going again, but the stories never changed much," Grandpa said. "I was always flaggerstaffed by such tales, even though I'd heard them many times."

"Flaggerstaffed, what does that mean?" said Ewan.

"He means flabbergasted." said Gran, "Always mixing up his words."

It was true; it was a trait in the family going back to Grandpa Coupar's own dad, who came to Port Glasgow in Scotland from Sweden to work in the shipyards along the Clyde. The story goes that during a lunch break he asked one of his coworkers what he was having for lunch. "A jeelie piece," was the reply.

"A jeelie piece? What's a jeelie piece?"

"It's just another name for a jam sandwich," said his coworker.

"If you have two words for everything, how am I supposed to learn your language?" cried Great-Grandpa. In learning this new language, Great-Grandpa would often create his own versions of words and this "tradition" was, perhaps inadvertently, carried on by the following gen-erations as new "Couparisms" continued to be added to the Coupar family.

"Aye well, next we'll be seeing the Bean-Nighe or the Banshee for the Irish kin, or maybe auld Black Angus, yon ugly auld dog, if this is true. But those are just tales," said Gran, looking wistfully at Ewan. "Dinna worry about them. We'll have a talk with Victoria."

"Who?" said Grandpa. "Who is Victoria?"

"Oh, just Billy's Grannie," said Ewan. "She's from the Hielands, too."

CHAPTER SIXTEEN

Faeriefolk Partners
(Part One)

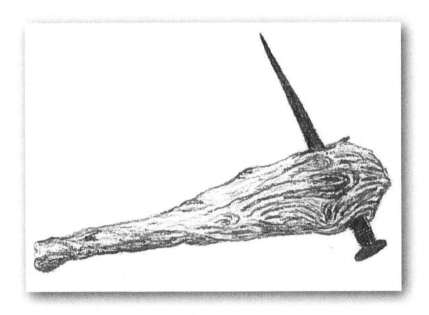

"You RECALL THAT story, don't you, Ewan?" asked Avril, bringing Ewan's focus back to the Cruach.

"Yes, I do, but so what?"

"So what, you ask? Well, first of all, I was thinking I would love tae meet this minister. How many times do you hear of a minister having a run-in with a Faerie, and this was a bad one," Avril said.

The others heard the news story, but it hadn't occurred to them to be of any significance. But now they decided they should find out if their parents or grandparents had heard of the Fachan. Leslie wondered if Shauna's Brownie or Pauline's Wag-by-the-Way or Billy's Draygan would have been a match for Peg Leg. Peg Leg apparently lost his club when it slipped out of his one hand, went sailing into the mist, and slithered down the mountainside with Peg Leg in hot pursuit. That was the reason given for no one being hurt. Peg Leg never returned, although he was heard muttering obscenities while searching. The fog eventually cleared, the hikers escaped harm, and a search was on for the club. So far, it hadn't been found.

"That's almost funny when you think of it, really," said Pauline. The scenario was hysterical by the time they all pictured a nasty wee Fachan losing his nasty club and the surprised look on his face and one eye as it went sailing off into nowhere.

"But still," Leslie said, "what if he hadn't lost his club? What would have happened to those hikers if he hadn't lost his club? They would have been killed, all of them. What would have been the explanation? He must be one of the bad Faeries."

"True," said Brian, "and it looks like we're all connecting this to us."

"Well, we'd be silly not to consider it," Belle said. "And if it is connected and if we get in the way, what protection do we have as ordinary kids? But I suppose we're not ordinary kids anymore."

"Some of our friends are pretty powerful, you know, with magic and all," said Pauline, thinking of the Wag-by-the-Way. "How powerful is your Brownie?" she asked Shauna.

"I don't really know," she replied. "But it seems to me we all need extra powers ourselves. If they can't be taught to us, maybe we should have bodyguards or something, like Billy's Draygan."

"He's not really my Draygan," said Billy. "I just know about them. With Shauna and Pauline, it's different."

"Is it possible we need that kind of help," asked Belle, "as well as learning some magic? Imagine me...I could be a beautiful witch with long flowing hair riding on a dragon fighting back evil."

Chapter Sixteen

"We should talk to Winthrop and Surston. I haven't even met Surston yet," said Ewan. "He would know. I feel like I want to wake up from a dream or maybe just find ourselves in a Faerie tale where we don't get hurt. What are we doing? How did we get into this?"

"But we are in a Faerie tale, and we are the heroes. We'll be fine, won't we?" said Belle. "Well, we will be, won't we?"

CHAPTER SEVENTEEN

Faeriefolk Partners
(Part Two)

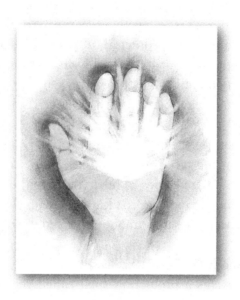

AVRIL FELT COMPELLED to speak. "I have tae tell you that since it's now been mentioned, I think maybe Surston and Winthrop will agree. We do need help. There are alternatives, though. You can be taught magic or, as I would put it, you can be endowed with some powers. But I think a partner for each of you would also be advisable, like a Faeriefolk partner."

There was a pause before anything further was said. Then, as if thinking at the same time, everyone seemed to say, "What about you?" It was uncanny the way everybody was beginning to think like one at the right time.

Chapter Seventeen

"I am a witch," said Avril. "I was born a witch. My mother's a witch. So I am better protected than the rest of you."

"Whist, whist, hold," said Brian. "Explain what you mean."

"Can you cast spells? Can you protect us? Show us something," said Shauna.

"Well, I was the first Ewan spoke to about all this except for his talks with Winthrop. You can't do that, Ewan, without some sort of gift. But before we get into all that, I really can't protect you just 'cause I'm a witch. I'm still learning, and even with full power we still need a Faeriefolk partner. This is…well…different. So, what can I do? I can cast some spells, and I can protect all of you for a short time. I can put halting spells on others, but I need help too. My mother is very power-ful, and she will help me. And by the way, we need to meet the minister. I think he's like us, maybe even with protective powers by the sound of it."

"What kinds of spells can help us that you do?" asked Ewan.

"I've been working on minor ones like this. I can give you a protec-tion spell so that if anyone tries to hurt you, it will backfire and hurt the attacker twice as much. So when you know someone is about to attack you, the attacker gets back the same amount directed to you without you being hurt."

"Show us something then," said Leslie.

"Let's try this. It's a protection spell called the Witherwillis spell," said Avril. "Leslie, you're the biggest and strongest, so I'll get Belle to slap you on the shoulder. You won't feel it, but she will feel two slaps on the shoulder. On second thoughts, let's reverse that. Leslie, you slap Belle. Belle, when you know you're going to be attacked, you say, 'Witherwillis,' and you will be protected."

"What does it mean?"

"It just means reversal or going backward or anticlockwise. It will work only for people of the Fae."

That done, Avril said, "OK, Leslie, slap Belle on the shoulder."

Leslie slapped her quite lightly.

"Ouch! That was a bit too hard," said Belle. "Oh, was I supposed to say the word?"

"Yes, of course. Try it again."

Leslie's hand came close, but just as it seemed to make contact, he felt two slaps on his back while Belle felt nothing. "Do it again," said Avril. Once again, Belle felt nothing while Leslie felt a slap. The others watched closely. Brian grinned at last, maybe realizing the significance. "So if I'm protected and somebody punched me on the nose, I wouldn't feel it but they would get two punches on the nose. Then if they tried it again, they would get two more punches on the nose."

"That's it," said Avril. "Whatever damage could be inflicted on you by an attack of any kind will backfire with twice the force."

Brian expanded. "So let's see, if I am attacked by somebody with a sword…"

"Same thing," Avril said. "It can protect all of you."

Pauline suggested a mission to search for the Fachan. "So if he attacks us with his club, he'll be in for a big surprise."

"Oh, I can think of lots of ways to try it out," said Shauna, "but I guess that's not the point, is it? We should keep these spells secret until we need them and not go looking for trouble and attract attention."

Avril looked knowingly at Shauna and nodded.

"I think I can count on Flamish and FireForge for protection, but what about the rest of them?" Pauline asked Avril.

"Oh, there are a lot more spells I can show you without the help of your own Faerie partners but I need tae know what ones tae teach you and not get in the way of your Faerie friends help."

Avril the Witch, it seems, had taken on a new role, that of teaching Faerie spells. "We must all find out just what powers we have. But Ewan's still the leader here. You must know now, Ewan, what powers you can achieve."

"No," Ewan said with surprise. "I never even gave it a thought."

"I know what I want," Brian said. "I would like to meet something from the sea, like a Selkie."

Chapter Seventeen

He asked if Billy could take him to FlipFloggle. "Could I become a seal myself by putting on a skin, or does it work that way?"

"We can find out," said Billy.

And so they started a discussion of Faerie partners.

CHAPTER EIGHTEEN

Faeriefolk Partners (Part Three)

AVRIL WAS ANXIOUS that each member of the Cruach find at least one faeriefolk partner. Avril's mother would be her protector, but she made it clear that she would remain unseen but close by her daughter for the most part. Avril's family generally kept their witchcraft a secret. With their combined power, Avril felt safe.

Chapter Eighteen

Pauline would be well served by Flamish and FireForge. The two flame-loving creatures were inseparable. If ever Flamish needed protection, FireForge was by his side.

Shauna, too, had secured herself a partner or two. Her family Brownie, Bonny Moon, had talked a Goblin, Gilnock, a cousin, into helping. Goblins were nothing more than disgruntled Brownies who loved malicious mischief more than helping people. When the situation was explained to Gilnock, he saw all kinds of opportunities to practice his pent-up tricks. He did see the dangers but was dauntless.

Ewan, becoming aware of his gifts, would see to it that he developed powers in a way that would work with his Pixie friends and Urisk friends. He and his three Pixies and two Urisks decided they made a good team. That and his contact with Rockkin folk seemed to offer most of the protection he would need.

"We now have Leslie, Billy, Graham, Brian, and Belle to look after." Avril gave a wee cheeky smile to them.

Surston, through Winthrop, picked the spot for another meeting, this time with the Cruach and whoever else happened to be invited. The locations were always interesting. Shielhill rose steeply just west of Loch Thom. The side facing the loch looked almost too steep to climb, but it was manageable. The top was flat and had a lip around the edge. It seemed as if it had been built up with earth. It well could have been.

Many Roman roads stretched from one spot to another in this region, and it was just south of Antonine's Wall. This wall was built in AD 140–42 and stretched across Scotland for thirty-seven miles from Old Kilpatrick, just north of the River Clyde, to North Berwick on the Firth of Forth. A road linked twenty-nine forts. The wall itself was ten feet high and fourteen feet wide, fronted by a twelve-foot ditch. The Romans used earth and stone to build such walls and forts, and Shielhill was high enough and flat enough for a Roman lookout fort or camp. Ewan pictured the armies of Scottish kings and heroes traversing this very area using the same roads the Romans had set. Indeed, this was just above the Shaw-Stewart Estate of Ardgowan Castle, which was given by Robert III to his son John in 1403. It was about three miles from the spot.

Winthrop had been waiting in one of the giant boulders within the earthen perimeter. When Surston appeared, together with Winthrop, it occurred to the nine that they had been here for some time with the two Rockkin in hidden attendance. But the Rockkin had been waiting for another being to announce her arrival.

It was another Sunday afternoon, always a day for a good excuse to be in the hills. The party this time had come to the loch by way of the cut, as it was called, a series of aqueducts to take water from the loch to Greenock. It was also a pleasant scenic path: trees and woods with patches of heather all the way up until it opened to heather hills at the loch itself. The weather was warm and sunny with a few clouds racing across the sky. It was always windy in this spot, but this was what Graham and Ewan particularly liked about it. Standing on the lip overlooking the loch with the wind blowing through their hair was like playing a song of freedom.

Suddenly, the wind stilled. "What's this?" said Belle.

"Here we go again," said Brian, who was sitting beside her. "It's just wee Faerie tricks, I suppose." Brian looked around, and the others seemed to agree with him. Mist swirled around them—above them but not among them or touching them. It turned blue, grey, and then green. Flashes of light, like small lightning bugs, shot around and above them. A throne appeared. The great high-backed wooden chair was dripping seaweed, and standing in front was a hag with dripping robes of saltwater and seaweed. It looked hideous. The Cruach gathered quickly as if in fear and in defense. A hollow voice said, "Oh no, that's not right." More swirling mist around and above them, more bolts of light, and the shape kept changing before their eyes. After a blinding flash, it all went back to the way it was—the natural clouds, sunshine, and breeze—but now sat a beautiful woman with long white hair and lacy robes of various shades of blue, some floating lightly away from her in the breeze. Despite the white hair, her face was young, almost as young as those of the girls. She was about twenty feet tall and was about to say something when she hesitated. She shrunk before their eyes to normal adult size with the face of an older, motherly looking woman. She fluttered her arms before her face as if to shoo away flies, lowered them to the arms of the large wooden chair, and said, "Well, good day to you."

Ewan almost pushed Avril ahead of him until she darted behind him, leaving him front and foremost. "Good day to you too," Ewan sputtered.

Winthrop appeared to his little flock and said, "May I present *the* Cailleach [call-y-ach]." This was the ancient goddess herself. The Blue Hag or Cailleach Bhuer, the Stone Woman. She went by many names and descriptions. Only Avril seemed to have heard of her and fell to her knees. They all looked at her and seemed ready to do the same when the Cailleach said, "Oh, get up, get up!" When Avril didn't respond, she rose five feet into the air, knees still bent. When her legs straightened beneath her, she was gently lowered to stand on the ground. The Cailleach rose and glided toward them and stopped among them. They formed a circle around her, and she looked at each one and said their names. She glided outside the circle and turned so she could view them all together.

"You can call me...um, Blue Hag. No, no, um...Miss Old Crone. No, that's not right either. Let's see, Mrs. Surston? Oh dear," she moaned until Avril jumped in. "May we just call you Miss Colleen? That means young girl, and it comes from an older Gaelic form of one of your names."

"Well, that's just what I was getting to until you beat me to it," said Miss Colleen. "You must be the witch girl. I'll bet most people don't believe you're a witch, do they? Witches are supposed to look like this." After a blinding flash, Miss Colleen was sitting on a broomstick five feet off the grass with a pointed hat, a green face, a pointed nose with a wart, and a long black gown. "Where's Toto?" she said, almost ready to grab Winthrop and enact a scene from *The Wizard of Oz* when Avril said, "Or this," and turned into the beautiful witch of the East, Glenda. They instantly turned back to themselves, and Miss Colleen laughed heartily. Avril heaved a sigh of relief, glad that she hadn't upset Miss Colleen with the witch exchange. It was obvious that Miss Colleen enjoyed it. Everyone's mouths were agape at Avril's boldness and talent. It was Surston who brought things back to what the purpose of the gathering was, and also realized that now the children were all staring at him for the first time.

"You will acquit yourself well," Surston told Avril, "but let's take care of the rest. Brian, Billy, and Belle," he said, turning to the three. "Here is what I propose. Billy, you are close to Carbost up there in the Isle of Skye and FlipFloggle and the sea. Brian likes the water ways for reasons of his own—fishing, I believe. Belle, it seems, is comfortable close to Brian. Belle, you do have the look of a Selkie child yourself. They may take favorably to you right away." Belle brought her hands to her face as if to hide a blush. Brian noticed that the skin between her fingers seemed web like. "Miss Colleen," said Surston, "has arranged a meeting with FlipFloggle, some Selkie, and merpeople. A wee visit to Skye as a holiday will help set that up."

Billy and Brian were obviously delighted with this idea, but Belle wanted one of the girls along. "You will have some female companionship. Never fear," said Miss Colleen.

"When can we go then?" asked Belle.

"Let's wait till school is out for the summer, and then we'll arrange something." Turning to Graham, she said, "What about you, young man?"

CHAPTER NINETEEN

Graham and the Wood Elves

Getting the chance to say something Graham piped up saying "I like trees. I like climbing the branches. The view from a tall tree is exhilarating. I don't know why. It's just something about trees I like."

Miss Colleen thought about it for a bit. "The Wood Elves, yes, you might get along well with the Wood Elves. They are a tree-dwelling spirit. They have powers they could teach you, but you must spend a good bit of time with them, and at rather specific times of the year, namely at the esbat—not always, but mainly."

"Ah, the esbat," said Graham, "which is…"

"That is the full moon, my child, the full moon. But once you have made friends, times are always easier. You must remember, too, that you have to be near trees to contact them. They can uproot and move around, but this draws attention, so they do so rarely. Lots of them can communicate through the roots of the trees they inhabit. You must find a nice wee spot with lots of trees, make a circle, and invite them in."

"Make a circle, what do you mean?" asked Graham.

"Of friends, maybe stones, or perhaps flowers. When the moon is full and all is quiet, you have to knock on a tree. Knock on wood. That's the way. You see where that expression comes from now. It's a modern superstition, but that's where it comes from. So knock to summon the Elves. You must look for a secluded, treed area, either with oak—that's their favorite—or willow, ash, or thorn, or perhaps rowan, birch, or elder. I will not tell you more, for you will experience something quite thrilling and relaxing if they come to you. I would advise the more the merrier of the Cruach when you do it. But make sure they recognize you as the summoner. Knock on wood. By the way, they were once a bit like the Rockkin," she said, tossing a side glance at Winthrop. "They used to be more humanlike but found a more spirit form of life suited them best. Trees gave them energy and protection, and in turn they gave the same back. They are also very ancient, and the Druids took much of their knowledge from them. Perhaps I should say that they taught the Druids. Good luck. I will be watching, but I will not interfere."

Nobody wanted to miss this night. The moon was full. A slight breeze moved the leaves. The spot was the entrance to the cut at the Loch Thom side. There were few human habitations nearby, so no artificial light disturbed the natural setting. The sheep were silent in the not-so-distant hillside. An owl was heard now and again, and the usual night sounds would break the rustle of the leaves in the trees. It was tree paradise. The Cruach had picked an open grove in the woods about two miles from Ardgowan Castle, an estate that itself was heavily wooded. The nine had formed a circle with Graham seated in the middle. Shafts of moonlight played around them as they sat in silence for almost half an hour. It was almost 11:00 p.m. Days were lengthening going into late spring, so the wait for darkness took them close to midnight. Finally, Graham said, "It's time." He had selected a tree a few feet away. He put his ear to it. "Hear that?" he asked. Nobody said a word. He stepped back and knocked on the tree, a large oak. He backed into the center of the circle and waited. He went back to the tree, knocked again, and returned.

"I forgot to ask…" said Leslie.

"What?" snapped Graham.

Chapter Nineteen

"How do you know there are Wood Elves living in any of these trees?"

Graham looked at Avril and glanced back to Leslie. "Trust me."

Leslie said nothing more. Just as Graham was about to try again, Shauna said, "Wait, what's that?"

"Its music," said Ewan.

"Nobody lives here," said Belle.

"Somebody does," Graham said with a smile. "Listen, it's harp music, or...sometimes it sounds like a flute."

Shauna sighed dreamily. "It's pretty, it's soothing, it feels...like magic."

Indeed, everybody was somewhat in a trance. The shafts of moonlight were being punctuated by twinkles of blue, then pink changing to purple, then red. It seemed as if a halo of pink light circled the entire outer rim of the Cruach as they sat stock still, not daring to move, frozen in anticipation. The tree Graham had chosen started to glow faintly greenish. It throbbed slightly, and there was rustling and movement about the roots. The rustling glided toward the circle, and Belle and Brian moved aside as if to let it pass in, but it stopped in the halo. It slowly moved around the halo in a counterclockwise direction. In response, the halo revolved slowly in the opposite direction. As if they sat on the dial of a large clock, the Cruach began to circle with Graham spinning in the middle. Faster and faster, until the trees were no longer visible beyond the circle and the moon grew brighter. Then everything was still. They were sitting on a large circle of pink grass. All around them, figures moved like the flickering northern lights. The music was coming from musicians and singers that were constantly changing shapes. Some played while others danced. A round tray for each of the Cruach appeared with a cup in the shape of a large outer casing of an acorn, filled with a dark-brown liquid. Cakes and other delicacies appeared in the shape of chestnuts, and a voice said, "Refresh yourself, refresh."

"Oh my goodness, I think we're underground," Shauna whispered.

"No, I think if you open your eyes you will still see the moon," said Belle.

"And the tops of the trees under this...whatever it is we're sitting on," said Leslie. "I can see the river and some coastal lights from here. We are very high up."

Graham, amused, stood up and said, "I think this is acceptance. I wonder what happens now."

"We talk," said a female voice. "We will talk to Graham through Layla. That is I. We will all listen and council you. We have names you will find easy to remember. We are Layla, Laurel, Leaffe, and Ladytree. We understand your plight. Imagine how we love the night or day, the fresh breezes to carry our music. It is from here, over and in the trees, we can help and use our powers. Graham, be patient, but meet with us frequently. Always be in touch. Till next time, then."

"No, wait, can I at least see you?" pleaded Graham.

"Why, yes. You are looking right at us." Graham realized that while he thought he was looking at trees he was actually looking at the Wood Elves. They looked very much like tree people, or people trees. Their arms and legs were like tree limbs and branches with leaves like hair hanging over smiling faces carved in wood. Their movements were graceful, like a breeze moving them back and forth. Then, just as suddenly, mere trees appeared again.

Ewan, Graham, and the rest had been talking, sipping, and nibbling while listening to the soothing music. After Layla's last words, all were soundly dozing. They woke up later underneath the trees with the moon still shining brightly. They felt refreshed.

"How long have we been here?" Billy asked.

"I feel like we just got here," Brian said, "but I know the moon has moved round a bit."

Graham said, "I think they're still in contact."

Avril agreed. "I feel like I can fly, and something is telling me to reach up through the trees—like this." She rose but appeared first as a translucent human form and then more like a ray of light.

"You can all do it," she called down. "Let's go!" One by one, they flew up and around and over the waters of the cut's winding path. As if by a silent order, they eventually alighted closer to the road to home. They stood and looked at one another with a kind of awe, laughing smiles, and bright eyes.

Everybody bade goodnight. Ewan's parting comment was that Graham had his partner in Layla.

Shauna, Bonnie Doon, and Gilnock

THE FAERIE PARTNERS had been established for the most part but not yet completed, and this was a concern for Surston and Winthrop. Billy, Brian, and Belle, the three Bs, would meet with their connections eventually in Carbost in the misty Isle of Skye while Graham, Avril, and Ewan were seemingly under the wings of their protectors, but there was still Leslie, Pauline and Shauna without Faerie partners. So Surston and Winthrop decided to help things along a bit and get things under control in that respect. Summoning the Cruach would become an easy task, when it was necessary. They would learn that when they were called together they would not be missed from their own world because while they were in Diterra, the lands in between, or the mists as it were, time was very different. What was a day in Diterra was but a second in the world of the Landerfolk, the human world, and they were never missed before being returned. So Surston and Winthrop decided it was time for Shauna to make a pact with her Brownie Bonnie Doon and his Goblin cousin Gilnock.

So, when summoned, Shauna exclaimed, "Oh what a surprise!" when she found herself suddenly in the presence of both Winthrop and Surston.

"But where are the others?" she asked.

It was always a surprise to Surston and Winthrop that nothing seemed to faze any members of the Cruach when odd situations arose unexpectedly, but they were getting used to it.

"Well we just thought that perhaps it was time to meet your Brownie Bonnie Doon and his Goblin cousin Gilnock. We would just like to make sure you are safe," explained Surston.

"Of course, I've already talked to them," said Shauna.

"But the others have not met them yet, have they? I think it would be good for the others to be there, like they were with Graham and the tree folk and with Miss Colleen" said Winthrop.

"Brownies and Goblins are not always nice with people they don't want to be with. They know me, but...I'm not so sure about the others." pleaded Shauna. "But if you think it's a good idea, well, we can try."

Surston and Winthrop both knew the surliness of Goblins and Brownies, but they also knew that Goblins and Brownies would know of any suspicious characters that had been around, and they seemed to always be aware of any goings on. Perhaps, just maybe, something would reveal itself through a meeting with them.

"Well, OK," said Shauna. "I'll talk to the others and Bonnie Doon and Gilnock. We'll do it if they agree." With that, Shauna was gone again, sent out of the mists, back to where she'd been.

It was not always that difficult to arrange these things when left up to the two Rockkin. And so a meeting was arranged in good time but in a somewhat strange location picked out by Bonnie Doon and Gilnock. The Cruach found

Chapter Twenty

themselves outside what seemed like an abandoned cottage from yesteryear, only abandoned because no present owners could be seen. But it did look immaculately well kept. It was a wee highland cottage, with whitewashed walls and a wisp of smoke escaping from the chimney above the thatched roof. Chickens roamed around the wee flower beds along the edges of the walls.

"Where are we?" asked one of the Cruach as they approached the front door.

"None of your business," said a voice from nowhere who sounded like he had a bad cold. "What is it ye want?"

"They just want to meet you both," said Shauna. "They're my friends and…"

"Just because they're your friends doesn't mean they are our friends. We can look after ye without their help."

"Och, just be nice for once. You know you can be," pleaded Shauna.

"Och, all right then, come on in," the voice said grudgingly.

The Cruach shuffled in and looked for places to sit down, which was surprisingly easy, for what looked like a wee cottage from the outside was quite spacious inside with lots of stools and chairs scattered around.

"Where are the owners?" asked Shauna.

"They are here but they don't see you. Remember ye are in Diterra." And immediately Bonnie Doon and Gilnock appeared.

"Oh, they look like Munchkins," said Belle. "They're so adorable."

"We are not Munchkins, you stupid child."

"You're grumpy."

"I'm not Grumpy either. I've never had anything to do with those seven cunning Dwarves."

"You mean that story is true? Was there really a Snow White?"

"Of course it's not true, well, sort of. There are seven Dwarves but the girl was just some village simpleton whom they managed to talk into looking after them and cleaning house for them." He paused. "I am Bonnie Doon, and this is Gilnock."

They both did look like dusty dirty versions of Munchkins, but if there was an "ugly contest" Gilnock would have won.

"We promised to look after Shauna and we will, having looked after her family for a long time now. But the real reason you're here is because of your two Rockkin types who are lurking in the background somewhere and want to know if we have any idea about possible dangers. Of course we do, that's why we know that they are here. Not much gets past our noses. Gypsies, beware of Gypsies."

Ewan let out an audible gasp. "I've heard something of Gypsies."

"Who's this English git you've got here?"

"I'm not English, and if you know so much you would know who I am," shot back Ewan. "But what about Gypsies?" he asked.

"Umm, fiery little buggar, aren't you? Calm down. Gypsies, well, here's what you need to know." Bonnie Doon and Gilnock spoke in short clipped sentences now, each finishing for the other.

Gilnock started, "Gypsies are travelling people."

Then Bonnie Doon said, "But not like tinkers."

"They do not come from Scotland or Ireland or England."

"But are people who spread through different parts of Europe."

"They travel constantly and are also, for the most, part of one large family."

"Tinkers fix things, pots and pans, farmyard equipment, and collect junk, including old clothes, and make them into something useful."

"Gypsies are not like tinkers. They have spells and magic of their own."

"And deal with mythical creatures that aren't supposed to exist anymore except in faerie tales."

"Sometimes their caravans are pulled by unicorns and sometimes by winged horses."

"They have strange music, not often heard in Scotland, played on fiddles and bagpipes."

"And they have exotic dances with exotic clothing and jewelry."

"They cast spells on people they don't like."

"And they collect information," finished Gilnock.

It was this last statement that hit home—collect information.

Chapter Twenty

"Do you always talk like that? I thought I was watching a ping-pong match. And information? Do you mean...from us, and for who?" asked Pauline.

Bonnie Doon answered, "'Twould be better lassie if they did not know of you and your little group, but it might be too late for that now. And for whom you ask? We don't know yet, but we can find out, and yes, we do talk like that when we're together; it confuses people but we are seldom together for the most part, for good reason."

"I've seen Gypsies in England when I was on the train coming up to Scotland, but not since then," chimed in Ewan.

"Pray that you don't, pray that you don't. But take heed of what we've told ye and I'm sure that your Mr. Surston and Mr. Winthrop will no doubt appreciate the knowledge, won't you sirs? Ye can count on us. We will keep a keen eye," Gilnock said, looking around knowingly.

Then, rather suddenly, Bonnie Doon and Gilnock were shuffling the children toward the door. "OK, meeting's over. Off wi' ye. Out ye go. Goodbye, goodbye."

Just like that the meeting was over.

"Harrumph," mumbled Surston. "Well, at least we did learn something, Winthrop."

I'm next, thought Leslie. When his head hit the pillow that night, he didn't realize how well connected he would be by morning.

CHAPTER TWENTY-ONE

Leslie and the Leprechauns

LESLIE DIDN'T REMEMBER how long he'd been asleep on his side. He was still relaxed from the previous hour's magic when he heard and felt something sitting lightly on his hip. "Psst..." He heard the sound and felt a slight weight on top of him. "Tunderin' begorra, he's a big boyo, this one," said a voice definitely Irish and that of an older man but slightly high pitched.

"Are they not all?" said another.

"Aye, indeed, but this one got a few inches on the rest I'll bet," said yet another.

Chapter Twenty-One

Leslie kept his eyes closed. He was slowly waking and realizing what was happening. His Leprechauns had contacted him. *This can't be. Where are the others?* Before he could think or do more, a voice said, "Stand him up then." Without further ado, Leslie found himself standing to attention with pajamas as his suit. He glanced around, scared almost to move his head, when a voice said, "Down here, me bucko, down here." The room was pitch dark, but the moment he moved his head, the room lit up to a height of three feet while darkness remained above. Five little people were staring up at him. He wasn't sure if they were smiling or frowning until they all started to laugh hysterically. "Would you look at that? Don't you just love the look on their faces, as if they don't believe their own eyes?" With that, they laughed more and started to dance, interlocking their arms and making lots of noise. "Shhh! You'll wake my folks," Leslie pleaded.

"Och, laddie, they're miles away." He looked around, and sure enough, Leslie was standing on the top of a hillside next to what looked like a cave.

"Well now, before you meet The Boss—he doesn't like being called the king, so sometimes we just call him Your Lordship—it's us you'll be with for a while. Wogglemuth, that is I, and yon fellow is Fiddlesticks, the fiddler." With that, howls of laughter echoed round again till he added, "And here we have Bones, and over there, Elbos and Clancy." They started playing. Fiddlesticks on his fiddle. Bones beat on a round drumhead with what looked like a real bone, while Elbos pumped and pushed his wee Irish pipes under his elbow. As if on cue, Wogglemuth went skipping into a jig and they all started dancing to their own music. The number of dancing men seemed to swell. All looked much the same, with red beards and hair, and wee green hats flopping around; jackets and trousers of green, red, and black, with silver buckled black shoes clicking away on the gravel pathway leading to the cave entrance. From deep inside the cave came a deep rumble, like the sound of thunder mixed with a hundred chariots rolling over the earth. The sound grew louder till the dancing stopped, and all eyes turned to the cave mouth. Mist came billowing out till it exploded. The rumbling stopped, and the wee army of Leprechauns stared silently. In the silence of the swirling mist stepped out the handsomest wee fellow you could lay eyes on, with shiny red hair hanging under a velvet green hat that appeared to have a gold crown attached to the brim.

"He always does like a grand entrance," said Wogglemuth, "so get used to it."

He had clothes similar to the rest of them, with a belly that pushed out a broad black belt fronted by a golden buckle. Over his shoulders, he wore a dark-green cloak fringed with white fur tied at the throat with a yellow cord and reaching behind him almost to the ground. He never even looked at Leslie, but his eyes roved about until they landed on the musical trio. He clapped his hands and roared with laughter. The music started up again as The Boss jigged his way toward Leslie, swinging arm in arm. From twenty feet away, he suddenly jumped, glided, and landed on a rock right in front of Leslie. Raised up now on the rock eye to eye, he bellowed, "Welcome!" He stuck out a wee hairy-backed hand. Leslie extended a hand and returned his greeting. The Boss stuck out his face closer to Leslie. "*Ciamar a tha thu*? [How are you?]"

"*Glè mhath!* [Glay-va; very good]," said Leslie, remembering a little Gaelic of his own.

"*Ceud mile failte*," The Boss said and added in English, "Let's away inside boyo." With that, Leslie found himself seated in front of food and drink for the second time that night. "I always like to eat and drink, so I do," said The Boss.

"I'm not very hungry, actually. You see, earlier tonight..."

"I know, I know," said The Boss. "But you can eat and drink what you like and never get full here, and all your favourites. The drink in this bottle," he put a large bottle encased in leather in front of Leslie, "is a magical potion. You will have some wherever you go from now on in our flask. It will last a long time, for all you need to do is wet your lips and lick them, and it will help you become invisible whenever you will it."

"So that's how you keep appearing and disappearing," said Leslie.

"Aye, and everyone thinks we're always drinking the whiskey to get drunk." Then he added with a wink, "There's a tad bit o' the truth to that." A loud burst of laughter issued forth, and the music and dance started up again. The Boss pulled Leslie off to the side. "Let's go back outside for a spell. Aha, excuse the pun."

"Do you have any idea where you are?" asked The Boss.

Despite the bare hills around him being well lit by a full moon, Leslie acknowledged that he did not. "Is this Ireland?" he ventured to ask.

"No we're still close to your home. This is atop of Misty Law Hill not far from Wemyss Bay and Loch Thom. We have our favorite spots outside of the Auld Sod, you know, and besides, Ireland is not our only home. This is about as high as we could find around here. This here, lad, is Clancy."

Clancy appeared in front of Leslie and in a singsong voice said, "Here's a hand, my trusty friend, and gie's a hand o' thine."

Leslie almost finished the verse as he stuck out his hand, but he then thought better of it.

Clancy said, "I'll be your...well, would you look at the size o' this for an eight-year-old! As I was about to say, I'll be your bodyguard. I'll be with you constantly. What's your favorite tippling? Ah, now, don't tell you drink only milk. Well, well, how would you like me to appear with you? I'm going to be your protector if you really need one. And why would you be needing one?"

"I don't know," Leslie stammered. "What do you mean, exactly?"

"Well, like The Boss has ordered," he turned and bowed to The Boss, "I will be watching over you and teaching you."

"Teaching me what?"

"Oh, things, things, you'll see. Now," Clancy said, "I can be a bird or, let's see, a...a...ach...well, we can figure that out later. I will choose for myself if I have to, but you just say, 'Whack fol the diddle,' if you want me to appear as I really am. Now, before the cock crows, we must end this meeting. Until next time, Leslie McMaun, till next time. Oh, and bye the bye, we are not cobblers and shoemakers. We are just little people like lots of the others, and we don't have pots of gold hidden away."

Leslie was suddenly back under his bedcovers with his eyes closed. When he ventured for a peek, there was a wee china Leprechaun sitting on his desk. It winked back at him.

With that taken care of and the Cruach feeling safer all around, next was Ewan's meeting with Surston to relate the news. Up to this point, he had met Surston only briefly with the rest of the Cruach, but now he and Avril would have a chance to talk with him.

Ewan and Avril wandered up the hill path to meet Winthrop and tell him about the Cruach when he found Surston already there with Winthrop. Surston appeared as he once was, much like Winthrop decided to do. He was a little skinny man with drooped shoulders and an unruly mop of white hair that blew about wildly in the breeze. He looked slightly bowlegged, but it was hard to tell in the faded brownish pants that fell just below his knees, topped by a cotton-type robe of a slightly darker brown. He wore, much like Winthrop, a rope tied around his waist more or less to keep his robes from blowing about. Ewan stopped to study him for a moment or two as Surston looked back at him.

"Oh, I know what you're thinking: not at all what you expected me to look like. Mmmm?"

Ewan was close to saying something when Surston asked, "How are your friends?"

"Well, we gave ourselves a name," Ewan said excitedly. "We thought that like King Arthur and his Knights of the Round Table who were on a mission, so are we. We are the Cruach. Avril came up with the name. To us, it means 'Circle of Friends.' And by the way, it is finally nice to meet you."

"Well, I must say the pleasure is all mine. I do like the name, that I do," said Surston. "Yes, I do. What are all your names?"

Before any of them could reply, Avril, who was becoming a bit of a shadow to Ewan, stepped in.

"Well, there's me and Ewan, Ewan's cousin Brian, Graham Austin, Leslie McMaum, Billy Maulin, Belle Aunders, Shauna McPhail, and an English girl called Pauline Marshal. Belle's real name is Isobel, but we call her Belle for short."

"How is your mother, Avril?" asked Surston.

"She's…umm…fine, just fine."

"Good to know. Do tell her I said hello."

Chapter Twenty-One

"I will," said Avril.

"Do you realize that seven of you have names that have the letters *au* in them?" Surston asked.

"Why, I never thought of that. What could that mean?" asked Avril.

"I really don't know, except that is the symbol for gold. You are full of surprises, aren't you? Maybe there is something to it, maybe not." Surston left it at that, except for commenting that the minister was due in town soon for a visit.

CHAPTER TWENTY-TWO

Mr. Gillanders

MR. GILLANDERS DID arrive in town as a guest speaker for the East Kirk Church in Greenock. He had been minister at the church for a while but had taken leave to explore other churches in Scotland, particularly those in the Highlands and Islands. The history of religion in Scotland was a tumultuous one, and Mr. Gillanders wanted to learn more about how the religions in Scotland were affected by, or affected, Druidism, Faeriefolk, and perhaps even witches.

He was invited to be a guest minister for the Sunday service as well as a speaker after the evening service, which the regular minister gave.

Owing to the recent publicity in the newspapers about the attack on Mr. Gillanders on Ben Lomond, in the mist with other hikers, the church hall was crowded. Ewan Colin Coupar was there with his Gran and Grandpa. Grandpa rarely went to such things, being more content these days with two or three trips a day to the Well Park to play chess or checkers with the other old men. But Grandpa was curious. Also in the audience that evening sat the rest of the Cruach.

Chapter Twenty-Two

Mr. Gillanders stayed on his chosen topic that evening, speaking about his travels around Scotland, even though most people wanted to hear about the Ben Lomond incident.

After the talk, as usual, tea and biscuits were served in the church hall. After answering many questions from the parishioners, Mr. Gillanders spotted Ewan next to the biscuits and came forward to talk to him. The crowd was thinning out, but Ewan waited a little longer till it was mostly just Ewan and the Cruach who were left. Mr. Gillanders cast a questioning look over them all, but his look took on a definite change when Ewan asked, barely audibly, "It was a Fachan, wasn't it?"

"A what?" said Mr. Gillanders, trying not to laugh.

Ewan said, "Grandpa told me."

Mr. Gillanders slowly turned his eyes to old Mr. Coupar and over the small group of children, obviously all in on this. "But how…what, eh, maybe we'd better sit over here." He indicated a table away from the few stragglers.

"Well, we'll away home now, son," said Grandpa Coupar, but Mr. Gillanders said, "No, please stay. This seems to be something you know of…this Fachan."

"Och well, it's just talk I once heard being told about…you know." Running out of something to say, Grandpa reached into his pocket for his pipe.

"I think I could go for another wee cup of tea," Gran said and made for the kitchen.

"So it's true," said Shauna.

"Course it is," said Avril.

"I see you're all in on this," said Mr. Gillanders. "Perhaps you'd better let me in on what you weans are all together for."

In turn, they told him the whole story about Winthrop, Surston, the Faeries, and the Cruach.

"What are you rantin' about?" said Grandpa. Turning to Mr. Gillanders, he said, "I telt him aboot the Fachan, but it's the first I've heard about all this…this Cruach. Not a word to your Gran, noo."

"Grandpa, ask Gran about Grannie Kempock and Victoria."

"So ye know," said Grandpa.

"Excuse me," said Mr. Gillanders. "I've discovered a lot on my travels and studies, but if what you have told me tonight is not just some made up...Faerie tale, well, this will open a few eyes."

"But Mr. Gillanders...sir, you can't tell anyone what we just told you. You understand, don't you?"

Mr. Gillanders put his hand to his chin and sighed. "So is this...the Cruach taking on members, and have I just been recruited?"

"I'm sorry, Mr. Gillanders," said Avril. "We didn't realize by telling you all this that...well..."

"That we would put you in this spot," finished Ewan.

"We just had to know about the Fachan," said Leslie.

"Besides, you'll love this. It's so much fun. Being in our group, you'll get to meet all kinds of Faeries," Pauline said in her English accent.

"Goodness, you're from England. How did you get mixed up in this... eh...Scottish ring of rogues?" asked Mr. Gillanders.

"Pauline. My name is Pauline Marshal. My family moved up here a while back. I haven't quite lost my accent."

"It won't take long," said Ewan, "but we all wish you'd keep it."

"Oh, and why didn't you keep yours then?" She laughed at Ewan.

"'Cause he's smashing without it, aren't you?" Brian said teasingly.

"Aw, shut it," said Ewan.

"That's no way to be talking," said Grandpa, "and in front of the minister, too."

"Well, I wish I were their age again," Mr. Gillanders said with a laugh. He turned serious again. "If what you say is true, what are your plans? Do I get to meet Mr. Surston?"

"I suppose you must," said Shauna. "But we just call him Surston."

"Of course, but if you all have a touch of the Fae, how do I fit in?"

"Well, what did you do when you saw that nasty wee beast come at you?" asked Belle.

"The first thing I thought was, 'This is great—at last a real encounter.' Then I saw the club and wished he didn't have that weapon and, fortunately, at that moment, it went flying."

Chapter Twenty-Two

"You did what?" said Avril.

"After that, well I…"

"No," Avril said, "I mean, you said you wished he didn't have the club, and was it just then it went flying out of his hand?"

"Yes, well, that was fortunate and timely, I suppose."

"But you wished it, and it happened."

"Oh, coincidence, it happens all the time."

They were all staring at him, half smiling and casting glances at one another.

"I wish that I could just wish, and as if by coincidence my wishes would come true," said Billy.

"Mr. Gillanders," said Avril, "if what you say is true, then…you… have…a…touch of the Fae."

"Well, we will test it at some other time. Sometimes these things have a time and place," Mr. Gillanders said.

Well, well, well, thought Mr. Gillanders, *this has been quite the evening. How does all this fit in and I'm a minister. Ministers are not supposed to believe in Faeries, but I do, and so did the Reverend Robert Kirk. He is responsible for my interest in all of this.*

"Mr. Gillanders, sir…" Before Billy could say more, the minister cut in.

"Please don't call me 'sir.' I'm just one of the group now, right?" He looked around at them. "Now tell me your names."

Avril introduced them all, including last names.

"Fair enough," said Mr. Gillanders. "That was easy."

"And you also have to meet and get to know my mum, Victoria, and Grannie Kempock."

"Grannie Kempock, the stone? She's a person…or what?"

"She is a Spirit of the Rocks, a Rockkin. Oh, you have a lot to catch up on," said Ewan.

"Indeed, so it seems. But you know, it is getting late and we will not catch up tonight. I'll return when I finish my lecture tour, and as soon as I do, I will contact you all and we can go from there."

Mr. Gillanders

Mr. Gillanders smiled as he watched everybody head out the door. In the back of his mind, the children were playing a joke of some sort. He wasn't sure if they were making fun of him and his recent adventures or...

As he was making his way to his car, a voice said, "You don't really believe them, do you minister?" The minister whirled around. After putting an unusual night to rest, he heard voices coming from out of the night with nobody visible.

Mr. Gillanders and Surston

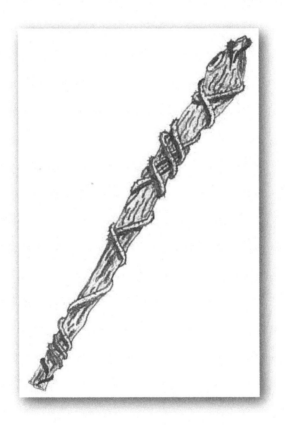

"I AM SORRY to alarm you like this. I could have been more tactful," he chuckled. "I'm Surston, one of the rock spirits the children talked of, and to get right to the point, I am fair intrigued by your experience, and you are a minister of the church. This must be confusing for you."

"No more confusing than voices from thin air. Where are you?" Mr. Gillanders was visibly shaken as he looked around.

"I'm here, and forgive me. I wasn't sure how to appear to you. I really haven't had much reason to appear before Landerfolk until recently." There he stood as he'd appeared to the children: a smallish man with an unkempt head of white hair and loosely flowing robes tied round the middle with a rope. The church parking lot was not well lit, and the minister was still wary as he noticed the long rod in Surston's hand. What looked like a Boy Scout staff wrapped with snakes turned out to be only vines.

"Well? What now?" asked Mr. Gillanders.

"I may be rushing you, but I was eager to let you know that the children are telling you the truth. This is a very unusual circumstance, and with you becoming involved, it leaves me with questions. Why and what enticed you to look into this 'mission,' this search for the Faeries? A minister going outside his faith..." It was Surston's turn to be startled.

"Robert Kirk. It started with the Reverend Robert Kirk. I read the essays of Robert Kirk, and that led me, out of curiosity, to his village, Aberfoyle. And I...well...I met him, kind of, by his tree. I went to Doon Hill."

The Reverend Robert Kirk was born in 1644. He is remembered for the accounts he kept in his essays *The Secret Commonwealth of Elves, Fauns, and Fairies* in 1691. Kirk had long been researching Faeries, and the essays revealed several personal accounts and stories from his local parishioners who claimed to have encountered them. Kirk grew up around Aberfoyle, where his father was the minister. Following his father's footsteps, he became a minister himself. He was first in the parish of Balquhidder until he took over his father's post as minister of Kirkton in Aberfoyle.

Kirk had long believed that the local Doon Hill, the Faerie Knowe, was the gateway to the Secret Commonwealth, or the land of the Faeries. It was a place Kirk visited often, taking daily walks there from his manse. The story goes that the Seelie folk and Faeries of Doon Hill allowed him on certain conditions to study them so they could be better understood. But the Reverend Kirk violated these conditions by going further into the domain of the Unseelie Court, where he had been warned not to go. His punishment was that he would be imprisoned in Doon Hill. One night in May 1692, Reverend Kirk went out for a walk to the hill in his nightshirt.

Chapter Twenty-Three

He apparently did this fairly often for a breath of air so as to sleep better. Some accounts claim that he simply vanished. Others say he had collapsed and was found on the hill and brought home, but died soon afterward. He was buried in his own kirkyard, although local legends claim that the Faeries took away his body and that the coffin contained only stones. The huge pine tree at the top of Doon Hill is said to contain Kirk's imprisoned spirit, but it's not old enough to go back to that time. Some believe it is part of the ever-changing tales of Kirk.

Kirk's cousin, Thomas Graham of Duchray, was then to claim that the spectre of Kirk had visited him in the night and told him that he had been carried off by the Faeries. Having left his widow expecting a child, the spectre of Kirk told Graham that he would appear at the baptism, whereupon Graham was to throw an iron knife at the apparition, thus freeing Kirk from the Faeries' clutches. However, when Kirk's spectre appeared, Graham was apparently too shocked by the vision to throw the knife, and Kirk's ghost faded away forever.

"That's the story, as well you know, I'm sure," said Mr. Gillanders.

After some moments, Surston said slowly, "You...met...him? Apart from the fact that you are both men of the cloth, so to speak, what prompted you to search him out?"

"I'm not entirely sure, but I do know this: he believed in his Bible, he knew the Bible well, yet had no trouble believing in the existence of the Realm of the Faeries and other dimensions. He just did not at the time of his disappearance understand how it all came to be."

"And you do?" asked Surston.

"Not entirely, but I am willing to find out."

"Mr. Gillanders, be careful. You know the fate that befell the Reverend Kirk for finding out too much. You and I have to talk. You will learn that this is all too real, and what may seem like a wee adventure tae these children is much more serious than it appears. You must keep an open mind. I do realize that so far it's been opened to more than you bargained for. Whether you see it or not, you must be...how shall I put it...involved somehow. Why or how, I don't know, but are you willing to find out?"

"Do I have a choice, Surston? It seems not, and I do know that this is all too real. So where do we go from here?"

"Then you know about the Seelie Court and the Unseelie Court, the big Faeries."

"Well no, not really. I have heard of them, but please explain. What's a big Faerie, and what's a little Faerie?"

"The little Faeries have existed on this planet, this Earth, for longer than I can know, for thousands of years. They are just that—little people but with powers beyond their human partners, the Landerfolk. They come in many forms or tribes, if you will. Going back as far as one can, they derived from a little race but took on slightly different forms as Picts, Dwarves, Brownies, Leprechauns, pygmies, and so on. They lived above the earth but became subterranean in an effort to survive, no longer able to defend their lands. They did indeed and still have certain powers, which Landerfolk call magic. On the other hand, we have the big Faeries, otherworldly beings that I will try to explain."

Mr. Gillanders realized they were not in the church parking lot any longer but sitting comfortably in his own living room in front of a warm fire.

Seeing the look on the minister's face, Surston waved his hand and said, "I can do these things. Get used to it."

Mr. Gillanders was about to say something when Surston raised his hand. "Maybe I should tell and show you all I know, and then you can tell me about your meeting with the Reverend Kirk, and we will both understand much more, I'm sure."

CHAPTER TWENTY-FOUR

A Long, Long Time Ago

"It might seem as if I'm treating you like a child, but it might be best to tell it to you this way. You see, a long, long time ago in a land far away..." Surston hesitated. "No, in a world far away, I mean not this world, but another world way out there."

He looked out of the window into the night sky. He looked back at Mr. Gillanders, whose only reaction was to look out the window and back to Surston.

"These otherworldly beings came in their vessels, these starships, looking for new worlds, for they were destroying their own. Ships made from materials not found on our Earth. These ships were damaged and could not return, so they and their crews were left here to do what they could to fend for themselves. They could not find the right materials to repair their ships. But the ships were not completely destroyed, and perhaps you can imagine the amazing things they carried with them. Their equipment and knowledge were so many thousands of years ahead of that of the people on Earth, thousands of years before my time. They also realized that returning to their own worlds was not possible. They had left because their worlds had been ravaged and destroyed by wars, and these otherworldly beings' differences were carried on for many more years here on Earth."

He stopped for a while as if looking for a way to continue. "I don't know of a way to tell you everything in such a short time, but know this. These starships still exist, and they are hidden away deep in their Faerie world almost in, no not almost, but in another dimension, or more like a parallel universe to ours. Am I making any sense?" Surston asked.

"You will need to go on; tell me more. I do understand somewhat about the Seelie Court and Unseelie Court and their secrets and desire to keep things that way. Kirk got too close and so…well, we know what happened to him. Please continue."

Mr. Gillanders was calmer.

"Ah well, good, I think. These otherworldly beings became the big Faeries of which the Seelie Court and Unseelie Court are part. The court is divided into two factors, as you well know. The Seelie Court is friendlier toward Landerfolk and to the little folk, the little fairies, but still they like to tease and sometimes torment. Some of the Seelie Court are called Elves here on Earth.

"The Unseelie Court, on the other hand, is not friendly at all. They are in charge of protecting their realm where the starships are hidden, and they do not trust anything or anyone outside their own realm. It is important that they remain hidden. These starships, if they are found by the wrong people or beings, would mean disaster. Old wars might rage again. Och, it's not just the ships but a vast amount of otherworldly knowledge. It's an evil intent that seeks them, and they have been seeking them for centuries."

"But who are these wrong beings you mention? Where are they from, and where are they now?"

"They are from other worlds—worlds from distant constellations where wars started before they brought them here. They are also big Faeries, I suppose, but do not quite see the allegiance as agreeable to them. In this world, as in other worlds, their greed and evil will not die. So the ships are being guarded by both the big Faeries of the Seelie and Unseelie Courts and the little Faeries by their alliance and by..."

"Well, go on."

"All this is being guarded and hidden away in another dimension—a parallel universe, if you will. Not easily accessible in this part of this world. They managed to create a kind of spirit world in between their existence and that of the little Faeries that includes all kinds of others like tree sprits, water spirits, and, wouldn't you know it, the Rockkin."

The minister stood up, slowly walked to the window, and looked into the darkness. He turned and, searching for words, said, "Look...I mean... who are you? And who is or what is searching for these ships? And how do they know of them?"

"I just tried to tell you. Did you not understand?"

"Yes, you did, and I understood some of it. But what does this have to do with me and the children, or do I still not understand something here? Is this a nightmare, and am I just dreaming?"

"No, you are not dreaming, and I'm not sure what this has to do with you or the children. That is what I need to know, and I will need to visit with the Faeries, all branches of them. I feel they will call on me soon. This recent visit by Aubrey and the Elves was a clue of something strange going on, but Winthrop and others of the Rockkin...well, we have been curious about Ewan and the other children, of course. Perhaps the next move is up to big Faeries, to let us know if their ships and their knowledge are in danger of being discovered, by whom and why, and what we can do to help fight this threat. They have been releasing some of their great knowledge slowly over the years, but they still feel the Landerfolk are not ready."

"Really, like what?"

"Well, just think how long Landerfolk have existed for years with-out the great magic of electricity, and then along come telephones and television, to mention a couple of things. Things like these were in existence thousands of years ago, along with much more amazing knowledge, but in turn they were used for destructive purposes. We shall see what the future brings. But now, I would like to know more of you, minister."

"Yes, yes, by all means. But one more question for now. If I was to gaze into the night skies, which I often do, where would I look? What constellation would I search for?"

"Ah, look toward the one known as Draco, or the Dragon. It is close by in the sky, at least as you look up, to Ursa Major, the Big Dipper. Its brightest star is Etamin, but there are many worlds out there, minister."

"I was wondering if you could perhaps stop referring to me as 'minister' and do as the children agreed to do and just call me Peter."

"But didn't they agree to just call you Mr. Gillanders?"

"Just so, just so. Actually, no, that's not it. It seems a bit unfriendly just calling me 'minister,' and you do have a way about you that is not endearing, if you know what I mean."

After a pause that was beginning to feel uncomfortable to Mr. Gillanders, Surston said, "Of course, minister. It's not that I was being disrespectful, because being a minister is a noble thing. I was, and maybe still am, in a way a minister myself. I was not being fair. I see that now. We must be friends, certainly. Well, we will work on that, and I will try to explain more as time goes on, and I will also get to know the children better to see what's behind all this. Now, I do wish you would tell of your meeting with Kirk. You can make it brief for now. Ah, but you did say you kind of met him? You haven't told me what you mean by that. Perhaps you should tell me more so I can...we can help each other here—and the children."

Mr. Gillanders realized that Surston really wanted to know, and truth be told, he was eager to relate it as much as Surston wanted to hear it.

"Well, it was my first venture into the unknown. I had read Kirk's essays, and what better place to start than Aberfoyle, so there I went."

CHAPTER TWENTY-FIVE

Mr. Gillanders and Robert Kirk

MR. GILLANDERS PARKED his car on the main street of Aberfoyle about a block away from the post office. What better place to get directions to certain spots he wished to visit than here? Since Mr. Gillanders decided to take some time away from his ministries to study Faerie beliefs in his native Scotland, this would be the place to start. For it was here that the Reverend Kirk apparently made contact as far back as the late seventeenth century and had written about it in his essays. This was what had piqued Mr. Gillanders' curiosity.

The post office stood on one of the corners of the main street—a two-story building topped with a round spiral turret and a weather vane. It was just afternoon when he approached the front door, turned the handle, stepped inside, and stumbled, not expecting a downward stair. Almost immediately, he had a feeling of uneasiness that he couldn't quite describe. He wasn't in the time and place where he thought he should be. He looked toward the counter, through the brass bars to the back, and was just in time to see a tall man—young or old, he couldn't tell—with long white hair and odd-shaped eyes.

"Hello," called Mr. Gillanders. "I was wondering if you could help me with some directions."

Instead of the gentleman, out came a middle-aged lady with grey hair and a smile pleasant enough to ease the minister.

"I was wondering if you could point me in the direction of Doon Hill and the grave site of the Reverend Robert Kirk at what they call the Kirkton Church."

"Oh, you mean the Faerie Knowe. Och aye, that's easy enough to do. It's a well-visited spot, and as a minister, you are probably a wee bit more interested than most other folks," she said.

The feeling of uneasiness returned, for Mr. Gillanders hadn't mentioned that he was a minister.

"They'll no' let ye in to the Knowe. The Reverend Kirk spoiled that for a lot of folk, and dancing seven times around the tree to see the Faeries will no' help. That's an auld wife's tale. If you sit by the tree, the reverend might want to talk to ye, but you'll have tae be patient. It's best tae go after six o'clock or so when it's quieter, and ye might have tae wait a bit, but that's fine. It's summer, and the days are long drawn oot this time of year."

She turned and walked into the back room. Mr. Gillanders felt an urgent need to leave and tried to utter a "thank-you." He opened the door and, before exiting, turned around to glance back at the counter, forgetting about the step up to the street level. He fell backward and landed on his backside onto the pavement. He felt rather foolish as a passerby helped him to his feet.

"If you're wanting to get intae the post office, they'll not be open till one o'clock; they're on their lunch hour right now." Addressing him was a lad of about eighteen years.

"But I was just in there," Mr. Gillanders said.

The chap tried the handle; it didn't turn. Then he pointed to the "Closed till one o'clock" sign.

"Are you all right? Didn't hit your head when ye fell?"

"No, no, I'm fine. I'll be all right. Thanks for your help. I'll come back later then." The minister made his way back to his car.

Now dazed and confused, he decided to check into one of the small hotels in Aberfoyle. This would give him time to settle and think, for he intended to stay for two or three days anyway. Once in his room, he unpacked a few clothes and reflected on what had happened at the post office. He thought about Kirk's reasons for looking for the Faeriefolk in the first place. It started when Kirk collected stories from the local folk about their beliefs. Mr. Gillanders wondered if there were many who still believed. Certainly what had just occurred was not altogether bad—just a little unsettling and maybe a sign that he should heed the advice of the post office lady, whoever she was, and go talk to Kirk.

I'll start at the post office, thought Mr. Gillanders. He vaguely remembered some directions the woman had given him.

Go out the door, turn left, and go a wee bitty till ye come tae the road that takes ye over the bridge that crosses the wee river yonder. That would be the River Forth. Then just keep on that road till ye come tae the church and the graveyard away up there on the left. Then go a wee bitty on again, and you'll find the path tae take you up tae the Fairie Knowe at the Doon Hill.

If he came out of the post office he had visited and turned left, he would be going in the opposite direction from the bridge road. *Well, to the post office then*, he thought. Much to his amazement, he found himself standing in front of a big house with a sign that said, "The Poste Cottage." *This is the post office as it was in the days of the good minister. Go from here.*

Unable to grasp what was in his head, Mr. Gillanders nevertheless did as he was bid and turned left from the old post office. He felt at ease in doing so. On crossing the bridge, however, he noticed that what he thought was a paved road was now a dirt road with not quite as many houses as before and of an older style. He continued till he reached the graveyard, smaller than he imagined, and to the wee church set off the road by about fifty yards. The door was closed at the front, and what a small door it was with a low stone archway. But then what a wee church it was with walls about two feet thick and windows on each side and a wee bell tower at the very back of the church roof. *Och well, it was a small parish.* Nobody was nearby except for a few birds flitting around. *I thought this was a ruin today,* Mr. Gillanders thought, but he felt pleasantly surprised that it wasn't. He paused for a while before wandering down and around the church to the back to view the Reverend Kirk's grave. There it was, but it looked fairly new as if it was only recent. *But no. That's not possible. It's not possible.* He ran his fingers over what looked like a newly carved inscription that read in part:

Linguae Hibernae

Lumen

M. Robertus Kirk

Aberfoile Pastor

Obit 21 May 12, 1692

Below the inscriptions was carved a square with a sword and something he didn't recognize. As if in a trance, he continued back up to the road and found the path leading to Doon Hill, the Faerie Knowe, and hopefully to Kirk's pine tree.

It was a pleasant wee stroll, although steep at some points. It wound around instead of going straight up, which made it easier to climb, but a man not in good condition could easily have a heart attack. He reached what was Kirk's tree. How he knew it to be the right one, he didn't know. No signs were posted as he would have suspected, and it was smaller than he imagined it to be—just a young sturdy pine surrounded by oaks. He wondered if the stories about the tree were true. If not, where would he find Kirk? But that voice that seemed to stay in his head told him what to do next. *Well here we are.* Mr. Gillanders knew he was not alone, not just with Kirk's spirit but others—yes, many others, but some almost as curious as he.

When seven o'clock came around, he found himself wandering around the tree site wondering if he was being foolish or just hopeful. He sat on a little grassy knoll near the tree and waited. *Is this really the tree that has Kirk's spirit or not?* After almost three hours, he was about to give up and go back to his hotel room when he heard a grunt, a "harrumph," or someone clearing his voice. He stood waiting for something more. Just as he was about to leave, he heard it. A voice with a distinct Highland accent was asking him why he had come and why he was leaving without as much as a wee chat at least.

"Kirk, is that you?" asked Mr. Gillanders.

"Aye, it is," came the reply.

Mr. Gillanders looked around. "How do I know someone here is not playing a trick on me and…is there any way you can…show me it's really you?"

"Och, I hope you're not expecting some Faerie magic; they would not allow that. They know you're here, so let's see now if they will…ah…do something."

After what seemed like an eternity to Mr. Gillanders, Kirk spoke again.

"Och, you are the lucky one. See now, it's well into the evening we are, but it's still fairly clear. Now wait a wee bit." As he spoke, a heavy mist surrounded Mr. Gillanders. This was not a normal mist but one that clung to him, enveloped him, and slowed his movements like he was in a big bowl of pea soup. He heard sounds, some musical metallic drums, tin drums, gongs, and bell tones.

"Do you ken where ye are now, Mr. Gillanders? Ye are in the Faerie mists, the land of in-between, Diterra. It goes by lots of names, Mr. Gillanders."

"The lady at the post office said I wouldn't see them."

"Och, to be sure you will not. She was right in telling you that. But she did let you know that I would enjoy a wee blether, did she not?"

"She did indeed. Ah yes, she did."

Mr. Gillanders was beginning to enjoy the situation.

"I have so many questions, but I can't think of one at the moment. This is beyond my wildest dreams for this to be happening. How are you, Robert Kirk? Oh, this is so…sudden. Perhaps we can talk a wee bit, and when I can, maybe I can come back again when I know what to expect. My mind is…how would you say…racing."

"Of course ye can, sir, but go now and explore what there is like I did and come back when ye are ready," said Kirk.

"No, no, wait. I am here because I read your essays, and I was curious. Why did you come to this place? You must have known something or someone would be waiting for you."

"Aye, to be truthful, I wasn't sure what to expect. I stumbled upon the Faerie Knowe by accident, or so I thought, only to find the guid folk had been watching me. I was made curious by the many stories I'd heard from the locals and them all the time telling me they were true. Didn't I know deep down inside that I believed them? So I went a-looking—much like yourself, I suppose. So here I am, and here you are, to be sure."

Kirk paused for a bit. "I have some regrets, of course, and I made some mistakes. I don't yet know what lies in store for yourself, but if I can be of any help in the future…just don't make the mistakes I made. Be warned."

"What did you do wrong, then? What mistakes?"

"I gave away their trust, exposed too much of their world. I thought I was bridging a gap between our world and theirs, but they didn't really want that." He paused. "Well, you know where I bide."

Mr. Gillanders was about to say something more, but the mist was clearing, falling away from him. He thought he saw an image being drawn away with the mist, waving good-bye as it disappeared. As one image disappeared, another came into view—a transparent female form holding out her hand to him. As he reached out to take her hand, she spoke.

"I am the keeper of the gate to this Faerie Knowe. We did not mean to let you get so close, and I know you are dazed. Let me guide you out of here," she said.

As he walked with his hand in hers, she continued to speak, but Mr. Gillanders could recall nothing more of what she said. Then she was gone, and Mr. Gillanders found himself back at the church. Now it was in ruins—no roof, no doors or windows, and gravestones now within the church walls itself. It seemed many graves had been added. The road back to the bridge and the village of Aberfoyle was paved now, and many more houses lined it. *I have been back in time.* The minister walked slowly back to his hotel room. Exhausted, he fell into a deep sleep.

"So that, Surston, was how I made the acquaintance of the Reverend Robert Kirk."

"Remarkable."

"I somehow think you knew that all along."

"I did," said Surston.

So it was that Surston and Mr. Gillanders forged a friendship and learned from each other while watching the development of the children's talents. Not much out of the ordinary happened over the next year or so as far as children of the Fae were concerned, although to normal folks some things would have raised a few eyebrows. To the children's credit, they managed to keep their adventures to themselves.

CHAPTER TWENTY-SIX

Camping

Most of their adventures now took place in the hills around Loch Thom. It was out of the way enough, yet there were many Faerie Knowes and cairns with underground streams, as well as old Roman ruins, roads, and forts. The mists were common, so visiting Faerie friends was easy but not without surprises now and then. It was the middle of the summer holidays from school, and Ewan, Leslie, Billy, and Brian were on one of their three-to four-day camping trips behind Loch Thom. There were four out of the five boys from the Cruach. Graham wasn't one of them. Graham was a member of the Boys Brigade organization, mainly because his father had been. Camping wasn't part of the Boys Brigade activities, and Graham wasn't really the camping type.

Ewan and most of his neighborhood buddies belonged to the Cub Scouts at the church across from the Well Park, about half a mile from where they lived. They had spent springtime weekends, when the weather permitted, at the Scout campgrounds with older boys, who were now in the Boy Scouts, learning about camping in general.

Chapter Twenty-Six

It was enjoyable for the most part, but the competitive atmosphere was not always fun for some. Ewan, on the other hand, enjoyed it. He was a member of the Cubs, who would one day be members of the Scout troop that was always in the running for the annual Everton Cup. The award was presented to the troop that was best in all the aspects of scouting from camp life, which included cooking, camp cleanliness, bridge making, and all kinds of backwoods stuff. Just about every Scout troop in the area, up to thirty or fifty, took part in the camp cooking, building bridges, following camp rules, making fires, and a variety of other things designed for survival in the woods and the wilds.

The camping during the summer months was altogether different. The boys had good camping knowledge, the sense of keeping a neat campground, and permission from the shepherd, Lachlan McLean, and his family. As long as they left the area as they found it, didn't set the moors on fire, and didn't disturb the sheep, things were fine. Lachlan and his wife agreed to sell them milk, eggs, and bread when they needed it.

With no agenda to follow, the boys roamed and explored at will on these trips. There was a lot to do up there in the hills: a hike from the campsite to a distant hilltop and back, or a swim out to the island and back, and every so often sheep in distress to be reported to the shepherd. There were many craggy areas and deep burns. Many sheep were lost, so Lachlan was grateful for the boys' help when one could be saved.

It was five o'clock one morning when Ewan awoke and looked out of the tent into a deep mist. He had never seen anything like this before. It concerned him but also excited him. Numerous sounds down toward the road and the loch puzzled him. He heard some cart wheels, horse hooves, and talking. The other boys were still soundly sleeping, so Ewan decided to investigate on his own. He slipped out of the tent in his shorts and T-shirt, and with bare feet made his way toward the loch. It wasn't that he was particularly frightened, for it could have been early-morning farm activities. He had heard farm life started early. He approached cautiously from a large grassy mound, over heather clumps and boulders, and down toward the road. The campsite was about a quarter mile up. The sounds were muffled at first, and Ewan would have to get quite close to the source to make out anything, the mist being so thick.

Camping

When he was about twenty yards from the road, he heard bagpipes, just a solo piper getting louder and louder until out of the mist came a ragged, kilted figure strutting along the road. Behind him was a small horse pulling a cart with an old lady. At least she looked old; it was hard to tell. She cradled a small child, and another sat in the back on a pile of assorted belongings. Walking beside the cart was a boy of about his own age and a girl about three years older. Well, this explained it—a highland tinker family on the move. There were many such families in Scotland still. In fact, one such family passed through the streets of Greenock twice a year, playing bagpipes and children collecting rags and stuff and throwing them into the back of the cart before moving on. It was an intriguing site. Somehow, this wasn't the same. Not feeling as apprehensive now, Ewan called out a greeting in Gaelic. Although he didn't know much Gaelic, he knew a few words, including "hello" and "how are you," but the words were hardly out of his mouth when everybody disappeared. The silence was so sudden that Ewan froze for a few moments. He didn't know that a mist, even one as thick as this, could swallow up sights and sounds so easily.

Ewan stepped back a bit and decided it was a good time to go back to the tent, if he could find his way. Between himself and the camp were a number of horses with riders thundering past him. He heard voices but could make out little of what they were saying and shouting. He could make out the clanging of metal and the thuds of hooves among the voices, but like the tinker family, it too stopped suddenly.

Ewan immediately thought of the story about his two grand-uncles and wondered if there was a connection. Was this another world up here in the mists, or was his imagination getting the better of him? He did and sometimes didn't believe the old family stories, and now he wasn't sure what he wanted to believe. He was scared and confused. It was still early, and perhaps he was sleepwalking. He found his way back to the tent. One of the other boys was awake and about to make a fire.

"Where were you? I was wondering if the Faeries had taken you," said Billy. "I called you, and you didn't answer. What have you been doing? Looking for breakfast?"

Chapter Twenty-Six

"Aye, and your calling wakened the rest of us. What are you doing up at this time? It may be light, but it's still too early to be up. My sleeping bag is still too cozy," came a response from the tent.

It wasn't long before everyone was awake and outside the tent.

"Are we in the same place as we camped last night? Something feels different," said Billy.

This put a knot in Ewan's stomach. His friends didn't know about his families' stories, but that was an odd comment.

"The mist makes everything feel different. Where else could we be?" said Leslie.

He's right, thought Ewan, *but something didn't feel right*. It was almost decided to pack up and leave because everyone was kind of spooked and didn't realize that this was typical. The sun would burn the mist soon enough. Soon, shadows shortened across the hills as the sun rose. The road could be seen snaking past the loch and far into the distance. If people had been near the loch earlier, the boys would still be able to see them. Nobody was on the road—no horse and cart, and no road they could have taken other than this one. They had disappeared into the mist, as did the other riders he had heard. Only Ewan knew this, and he was beginning to believe the crazy family stories.

"I've got some good stories for tonight's campfire," Ewan said.

That was how they spent the hour or two at night around the fire, either singing or telling stories. It was easy for young minds to make up new stories, but nobody believed many of them. Would they believe Ewan's story tonight, even if he swore up and down it was true? What about tomorrow morning? He was half hoping it would happen again, and he would wake them all. Then again, he was half hoping it wouldn't.

During the day, Ewan noticed odd patches of mist developing over certain parts of the hills. He had a feeling that after his nighttime stories were told, he would surprise or offer a unique experience for his friends in the morning. Ewan thought of casually engaging Lachlan in conversation about the misty mornings, although he couldn't think of why that had come to mind.

CHAPTER TWENTY-SEVEN

Ewan's Campfire Story

THE DAY WAS spent just exploring different areas around the campsite, looking for possible hidden caves or openings in the steep sides of the main creek that made its way down to the loch. There were no stranded sheep to rescue, so no visits to Lachlan were needed today. Ewan had lots to think about but had not shared his experiences of the early morning with his friends. When the sun went down and tent sites were lit by campfire, and cocoa was in order, it seemed as if everyone was too tired to think up new stories—everybody except Ewan.

Chapter Twenty-Seven

The other boys were happy to settle back and listen. Ewan started. His great-great-grandfather, from his father's side, that is, had come across the sea from Sweden, or so he said, but his grandchildren recalled his stories about flying across the sea from the east and landing in a great mist on the land in which there were Picts and witches.

"But how did he fly? There were no airplanes back then if it was your great-great-grandfather. And what part of Scotland was it if there were Picts and witches?" asked the boys.

"I didn't say it was Scotland, but it was. I think it was Tarbat Ness. He told strange tales about a mission he was on and got lost on the way. There were great tales he had written down, but he eventually acknowledged that he had come by boat to Scotland and settled here with his Scottish bride from the Highlands. Yet he often maintained his first story was true to certain close family members. But there was something in his memory that kept coming up. As years went by, he often wondered just what had happened—strange lost memories of a mission unfinished. He was long dead now but had many children and apparently made some kind of impression for them to remember and pass on the story of his coming to Scotland, for maybe one of his children or grandchildren was destined to finish the trip."

"Are you just making this up, or is this true do you think?"

"I don't know. I'm just telling what my grandpa tells me sometimes. He's a good old storyteller, my grandpa," said Ewan. "Oh, and he said there was a mist. Most of the time there was the mist. Don't forget about the mist. That was in the mid-1800s, and time wore on, and the old man died before the turn of the century."

"And there's more," said Ewan.

He went on to tell them that after the great war of the second decade of the next century, the story took on a new life among his family. It seems one of his grandsons, Claud, loved to walk in the hills behind Greenock, which at that time was fast becoming a popular seaport and shipbuilding town. Claud had worked in the yards and the same part of the river as his father had worked, mainly rafting logs that had come from Canada upriver and left to season in the salt tide before being cut up and used for building ships. In between loads, he had days off. During those times, he took advantage of the open hills above Greenock. It appeared that after a period of doing this, he would disappear for more than a day or so. After returning unharmed and none the worse for wear, his family stopped worrying about him and thought maybe he was spending time with some secretive friends or perhaps a young lady. They preferred to believe that than the stories he hinted about, concerning the mist, the Roman road, and some kind of other world. But his elder brother, Charles, was very interested in these stories. Claud did not drink, but Charles liked his daily draught and Scotch after he finished work. Charles stoked coal on one of the new river steamers, The King Edward, which took passengers to destinations up and down the river and the coast. It was almost a solitary job down there in the boiler room, but Charles liked it that way. He was a bit of a hermit himself and liked his one spot in the local pub he frequented after his river voyages. The publican knew what Charles liked, and when he arrived the publican would send back his draught and Scotch to the corner, where nobody bothered him. The locals knew Charles to be a bit of an eccentric, so they left him alone. Brother Thom would come in once a week and pay his bills. So Charles had little or no contact with anybody. On hearing Claud's stories of the mist, he seemed to be the only one who believed them and talked Claud into taking him one day without letting the rest of the family know. That was the last anybody ever saw of them.

"So there you have it. My great-uncles might be wandering around up here somewhere in these mists," said Ewan. "I, or we, might even meet them sometime this summer."

He told them about the events of the early morning. It was a good story up to that point, but when the truth sank in with the other boys that what he was telling them was true, they stared with open mouths for a few moments. Then broad grins broke out in the light of the fire, and they congratulated Ewan for coming up with a good one. Ewan didn't grin back but kept a serious face until the others realized he was trying to tell them he wasn't making this up, at least not about the morning episode. Ewan explained that he hadn't really believed the family stories until now. Nobody knew what to say for a few minutes. Ewan asked if anyone else had seen

Chapter Twenty-Seven

misty patches throughout the day come and go rather quickly. It had been a warm, sunny, cloudless day in the hills, but they all seemed to remember some wee misty patches whisping around. They started to look beyond the fire's light as if something or someone was out there watching and listening to them. Now and then, a wee bit of fear would grip them and the idea came up that perhaps leaving now, even in the middle of the night, would be good. But no, an adventure was waiting to happen—maybe as soon as the morning light approached with a mist.

CHAPTER TWENTY-EIGHT

The Boys Go Into the Mist

THEY GOT LITTLE sleep that night, as they wanted to be awake at the right hour just in case. There was lingering apprehension because maybe Ewan had just spun a good yarn and was still laughing inwardly. They kind of hoped it was true. But by the early-morning hours, they couldn't stay awake any longer. As they lay sound asleep, the silent mist enveloped the tents.

A sudden noise from outside the tent jolted everybody awake.

The tent flaps were opened, but nobody went outside. They just peered out and listened. Thick morning mist in the hills wasn't unusual, but after Ewan's story, this one was different. Or was it? After a few more minutes and no more sounds out of the ordinary, the lads thought about curling back into their bags but decided to venture out instead. They wanted an adventure, after all.

Chapter Twenty-Eight

Dawn hadn't arrived, so the boys needed torches. The site was situated beside some boulders purposely, so some natural seating was nearby. It seemed at first glance as the torchlight beam scanned the site that a couple of figures were occupying two of the boulders. Brian dropped his torch and grabbed Leslie, which made him drop his. Amid gasps, a voice said, "We're sorry, we're sorry. We didn't mean to startle you."

It was a female voice, soft but reassuring.

"We met yesterday, but you surprised us and we didn't expect you to be up and about this early."

Lachlan, the shepherd, had risen early that morning as usual and waited till the morning mist had cleared. He eventually wandered over to the boys' camp. He hadn't visited them since he saw them set up camp three days earlier, but they had been camping here two or three times this summer, and they knew his rules. He wasn't checking up on them but just wanted to say hello. The tents were open, sleeping bags still spread out inside, no morning fire, and no boys.

Lachlan pondered the empty tents and empty campsite and wondered if he should be concerned. He looked to the loch and the island. There was no sign of fishing or swimming, but something told him things were fine. He looked to the hills and thought what a beautiful day it was and that the boys were probably high up or over to Cruech Hill. He remembered Ewan's fascination for cairns, and several in the area were within hiking distance. One was as close as a stone's throw, and a little farther east in the small forest was another. He knew the boys had been to both of these, so perhaps now they were off to the Corkney Top cairn or Knockminwood Hill cairn. Perhaps, because they had apparently left so early, they might have decided to explore the legend of the Laverock Stone or check out the Grouse Railway tracks beyond. What he didn't realize was that the boys were sitting a few feet away, in Diterra, the land in between, talking to a tinker family. He didn't hear the pipes or the laughter. He eventually shrugged and smiled, for he knew a thing or two about what could be happening. He left, for he had things to do.

A figure rose from one of the rocks and approached the tent.

"When you called to us the other morning, we were startled."

Now the tinker family was once again standing before them. What Ewan originally thought was a boy of his own age was actually a girl, about two years younger than him, and her sister one year older than Ewan. They referred to their mother as Ma and father as Da. Two elder brothers and the baby made up the rest of the group.

"We have been granted passage through Faerieland for many years now," said the girl. "They allow us to exist both in our old world and here, in Diterra. The Faeries, that is. But we stay here mostly. We were displaced from our Highland home many years ago, and where sheep now graze we are no longer welcome. Many of our friends left for other lands while others like us chose life in the Lowlands. It did not suit us, so we have wandered ever since. The Faeries took pity on us and others like us, but our tinker life serves us well, and we live well in the land of the mists with the Faeries."

"But how old are you?" blurted Billy.

It wasn't exactly what any of the boys was thinking, but that was the first thing that came out of Billy's mouth.

The younger sister answered, "Well, Da was born in 1800, Ma in 1810. They got married in 1835. James and Charlie, the twins, were born in 1836. My sister Bridget was born in 1838, and I in 1841. I'm Mary, by the way."

The singsong accent of their tongue was like a spell on the ears of the boys. A Highland accent was something not altogether common to them.

"I'm…uh…Billy, and this is…well…Brian, Leslie, and Ewan. So you're not real Faeries, then? We've been keeping company with the Faeries but didn't know that real people lived in the land of the mists with them."

"I just told you about my great-uncles, did I not?" Ewan said.

"Aye, you did, and now we believe you," said Leslie. "What now?"

Mary turned to her twin brothers and said something in Gaelic. "Would you be wanting to hear a wee tune on the pipes, then?"

"Yes, but in a wee while. Some questions first. Maybe you're used to it, but to us you're over one hundred years old," said Leslie.

"This is an awful good trick," said Brian. "I like a good trick."

Chapter Twenty-Eight

"But it's not a trick you're seeing," said Mary. "Would you *like* to see some magic?"

"Careful now what you promise," said Ma. "We don't really have the magic ourselves, but if we ask the Faerie folk for something, maybe they will show you."

"Aye, they will or they would not be letting you in," said Da. "One of ye or all perhaps must have a touch of the Fae."

"What does that mean?" Billy asked.

"It means," said Ma, "that perhaps ye have some Faerie blood. You know, maybe somebody in your past was married to a Faerie. You are kin to the Fae Folk."

"Och Ma, you're always looking for that, but were we not chust kind to them many's the time."

"We've no Faerie blood at all, at all," said Da.

"But did ye not chust say yourself that they must have a touch themselves to be here?"

"Aye, I did that," said Da. "Och well, could be you're right, but I think we do too. It chust stand to reason."

As they were talking, the loch had disappeared and the landscape changed a bit. More trees appeared, and Ewan, Brian, Leslie, and Billy stood up and turned around to look as wee Bridget pointed to where the loch had been. Ewan looked toward Lachlan's place. It was also gone.

"What's happening?" said Leslie.

"Well, ye asked for a wee bit of the magic," said Mary, "and, well, I think we are not where we were in time."

"But what—where—or when is this then?" asked Brian.

"This must be up here before the loch was developed years ago. You know the loch is man-made," said Ewan. "So are we back in time? All these trees used to be here, and there is a wee stretch of water down there."

A cold breeze blew over, and like a cloud covering them quickly and disappearing again, the scene was back to normal.

"That's all the Faeries want you to see, I suppose," said Ma. "They're not ones to trust too much."

"I think we've seen enough for now. Will we get a chance again?" asked Billy.

"Who knows, who knows?" said Da.

"We're up here quite a lot," said Leslie.

"You don't have to be just here—just whatever or wherever, if they let you. We spend most of our time traveling, and it makes no difference where we are," said Mary.

Like most other things, it was over too soon—but not before a few tunes by James and Charlie and some laughter. Lachlan heard nothing as he walked back to the farmhouse, but on looking back, he could see them all standing around talking excitedly. *Where did they come from all of a sudden? Funny that, ah well.* He got on with his chores.

CHAPTER TWENTY-NINE

The Dream While Camping

THE NEXT MORNING, an early mist had come and gone, and it was beautifully clear again. It was still early, and coolness lingered. The boys had risen early enough and cleaned camp after breakfast but showed no real signs of making any solid plans for the day. There had been no breakthroughs to the people of the mist this morning, so they were feeling disappointed.

Ewan pulled a sleeping bag onto the grass and lay in the sun face down until some plans were made for the day. He soon fell into a deep sleep. Whether this was a dream or some omen in the form of a dream, Ewan wasn't sure. By the time he awoke, it felt like a warning. It started as a feeling of foreboding. An unknown evil force seemed to be creeping up. Then it took on the form of an invisible giant with thunderous footsteps getting closer. It was too incredulous to grasp. Then, like falling from the sky and falling away forever and ever, counting endlessly. He awakened in a panic but did not move for a few minutes, till he was able to roll onto his back and open his eyes. The first thing he saw was a skylark high above him, hovering in the sky against a blue background, before it plummeted after an insect and disappeared from sight. This brought him back to reality and helped shake the feeling of terror. He put it all down to falling asleep in the sun and hoped he would be able to forget it. He looked back into the sky and across the hills expecting to see a monstrous giant looking toward the camp, but there was nothing but calm now. He could not shake the feeling that this was a sign of evil to come, but from whom and why? None of the others had noticed his discomfort, so he kept it till later and wondered how to ask if they had any similar dreams. At least it would be something to discuss around the campfire.

He jumped up and shouted, "Is anybody ready to do anything?"

"Last time I looked in your direction, you were sleeping. Didn't want to wake you," Leslie's said. "Billy and Brian are down at the loch checking the bites for fishing later."

Ewan didn't feel like fishing.

"Let's just go down and throw some skiffers in the water, and then we can see if there's something interesting to do later," said Ewan. He needed to do something to take his mind off the dream, and that seemed perfect.

"OK," said Leslie, dumping an armful of wood and thankful for something else to do.

"But no racing down. I'm not up to it." So they casually strolled down to the loch's edge to join the others.

CHAPTER THIRTY

Ewan's Dream

It was later that week when Ewan saw Avril again, but he lost no time in asking for her opinion.

"Avril, do you ever dream?"

"Of course I do. Why do you ask?"

"Do you remember what you dream about?"

"Sometimes, but not always. Why do you ask?"

"Well, I've been having these dreams for quite some time now, and it wasn't until I had about three or four of them that I realized the dreams were connected. One after the other, and now I've dreamed about twenty, I think, and there seems to be a story to them. The funny thing is I have other dreams also, most of which I cannot remember, but these connected dreams I remember well."

"I know you're going to tell me about them, so why don't you start now?"

Ewan's Dream

"The first one is about a king, a long time ago, who rules a vast land, and he has two sons. When he dies or goes away somewhere—I'm not sure which—the elder son is supposed to rule in his place, but the younger son doesn't agree. To appease his younger brother, the elder brother agrees to let his younger brother rule parts of the lands to see how he manages. The younger brother is still not happy about this arrangement and makes plans to take over the land. I'm just a bystander up till now, but the dream takes a funny leap. When the elder brother becomes aware of a possible war, the solution is far across the sea, and he must send a traveler to find it. This is where it seems I become part of the dream. The traveler they send across the sea is I.

"I'm not, by the way, telling you each dream separately. I'm just filling in the whole story. Anyway, this traveler leaves from a cliff overlooking the sea with some other counselors around him, and he is told to fly over the sea, and use some sort of compass or other guiding tool to help him find the people who will advise him. He can fly by his powers of concentration, kind of like levitating, until he drifts like a cloud over the sea to a distant shore. The problem is, when he gets tired, he starts to lose the powers of concentration and has to land and rest before he can fly any further. He does have enough strength to reach the distant shore.

"The first place he lands is a river that flows into the sea, but there are a lot of little lakes and ponds around it, where he rests. When he awakens the next day, he gets the feeling that he is being watched. Well, he is, and the things that are watching him are from the ponds and the river. They look like human beings turned into fish. They have arms, legs, bodies, and heads, but they are covered in scales and have fishlike eyes and mouths, with gills on the sides of their necks to breathe when they're underwater. He feels that they should be contacting him. They are not scared of him, but they don't want to come close. They decide not to make contact. He continues on his journey without talking to these fish people.

"The next place he lands is in the middle of a forest. It has a clearing with two rows of cottages on each side, kind of like a village with a road in the middle. The cottages are made of wood and no more than two stories high, but they have all kinds of moss and other vegetation growing over them. They looked like they were uninhabited with backyards and sheds or stables behind each house. No flowers or other pretty things to look at—pretty dismal feeling in all. The cottages were all kind of dilapidated, with no windows. When he gets to this street, or more of a dirt road, he notices a lot of scruffy, skinny women with ragged clothes and old looks. It seems they were trying to entice him into a cottage so they could capture him. Some men appear who were just as ragged but scared looking. But they want to help him, and take him to the back of one of the cottages and lead him through the backyards and gardens till he's on the outskirts of the village. They tell him to be gone for his own safety. There is no explanation for all this, as he just listens to them and flies farther away.

"After flying for some time, he notices in the distance a huge dome. It looks like it's made of glass or maybe like a big soap bubble, and it covers quite a large town. It is hard to say what period some of this stuff is happening, but it looks like kind of a modern town—stone and brick buildings, shops, and street people. He doesn't want to call any attention to himself, so he flies under the dome so he can get a good look at the place. He tries to stay out of sight but is eventually noticed by a lot of the townspeople who were all looking upward pointing and shouting as he drifted around, kind of looking like a cloud but obviously a human being at the same time. He does not want to land there, as he has a sense of apprehension, so before he gets too tired and loses his concentration, he decides he'd better leave. They do not follow him because they seemed reluctant to leave the perimeter of the town, and he drifts away wondering who they were and what the town was, but feeling he was better to avoid them."

Interrupting the story, Ewan said, "Oh, by the way, I forgot to tell you that as the traveler was leaving the cliff top to fly over the sea, he was given a wooden compass."

"Yes, you did tell me that. Has he been using it?"

"Yes, he has been using it. He puts it into water, and it points to the direction he has to go to next."

Ewan continued the dream. "After the domed village, he eventually stops that evening to rest, and he meets a kind of strange underground people who takes him into a big cave and tells him they were expecting him. They feed him, although apparently they do not eat like normal human beings. He was in the presence of Faerie-like beings, who did not need a lot of sustenance or food to keep them going, almost like himself. They took him into their big cave under the ground. It looked like another world altogether with strange lights coming from different places. Other people were in there, of all different shapes and sizes and looks. They told him that they knew why he was there.

"He noticed a lot of strange-looking vehicles and things that looked like weapons—ancient weapons and vehicles that he didn't recognize. They took him to another cave within the cave, and there were what looked like thirteen swords suspended in midair with no visible means of how they were being held up. They all pointed downward. They had this strange glow, and he was told that the answers to his questions were to come from the swords. The questions required yes or no answers. If the answer was yes, then the swords would glow. They'd kind of vibrate and make singing noises, almost like chimes. If it was a negative answer to the question, they would not respond whatsoever. He didn't get anywhere with this and was confused. He stayed a few days but decided after a while that he was getting nowhere and needed to continue his journey to the next stage. There was no objection to letting him go, with apologies that they couldn't help him, and perhaps he'd come back this way in the future. So he rested, got his directions from the wooden compass, and left one morning. He flew and floated all day in the direction the compass gave until midevening.

"He found a spot and lay down to rest out in the open hills. When he awoke in the morning, he found himself surrounded by a lot of earth people, humans."

Again, Ewan interrupted himself. "I should've mentioned earlier in the dreams that he was not really a human—more like a Faerie or an Elf or somebody else with strange powers. Obviously, if he could fly, that would be a clue."

Ewan continued with the dream. "These people didn't treat him badly, but they took him to a village with a big castle in the middle of it. The village had lots of small houses and streets around the castle. They didn't talk much, just asked what he was doing. Later on in the day, they put him into a kind of prison, like a dungeon, although it wasn't the kind of dungeon that was deep down in the earth. It was like a big slab of stone, long and narrow, and down the middle of this slab of stone a stream ran. The stream came in through one end of the dungeon or prison, ran for about one hundred yards or so, and then exited like a waterfall on the outskirts of the village. Other people were in there—not like him, but more likely villagers. Although they weren't being treated badly, they didn't want to be there and were looking for ways to get out. Oddly enough, one of the other prisoners was expecting me, the traveler, and took me aside," Ewan said. "Remember, I told you in the dream that I was the traveler.

"This other prisoner told the traveler that there was a way out and they would all go together. After their escape, the two of them would meet up farther down the stream. The plan was simply to go into the stream, let the current take them over the waterfall, which was not high, and they would be carried down until they were far enough away from danger and meet up to talk. Well, that was what they did. Simple enough, everybody jumped into the stream and floated away with the current over the waterfall and stream, cascading down through the hills. There was a chase by some of the guards and some of the other people in the village, but everybody seemed to get away. Then the traveler met up with his newfound friend, who told him he would be able to help them on the next stage of his journey.

"He took the traveler to another castle, where he was given directions to go to meet up with somebody else who would explain to him just why he had been sent on this trip and would take back some information. He was warned that he would run into more dangers before his final destination in this land. The last place he would reach would be known as the Glen of the Evil One, on the banks of a great river. He was not to be scared of the being that lived in the glen. The evil one was not really evil; only the people who lived in the area were scared of him, and that was the way he wanted them to be. For he was not really a human but something like a Faerie spirit."

Ewan said, "The dreams to me are sometimes confusing, but that's the way I dream them."

"After the traveler reached his destination of the Glen of the Evil One, he got the information he needed and left to go back to his homeland."

Ewan looked at Avril. "Unfortunately, my dreams didn't tell me anything about this so-called Evil One and what information he was given. I haven't had another dream for quite some time now, but I suspect it all has to do with the Realm of the Fae and our odd adventure. I think we should talk to Surston about this. Do you think any of the dreams have to do with Surston and the others, or are they just a bunch of silly dreams?"

"Wow! That's quite a story, and all from dreams," said Avril. "Yes, I would think we should tell Surston just in case there is anything to them. When did all this take place? I mean, in all these dreams?"

"I have no idea," said Ewan, "but I do know it was a long, long time ago, and I think the traveler came from Sweden, but before it was Sweden, and he came to Scotland, and then went back to Sweden."

"I think we should tell Surston, and perhaps when you're telling him I can be there," said Avril. "You might remember more."

"I might, but I think I told you most of what I can remember, and if there is some meaning to the dreams, then Surston, who is also very old, may be able to tell us what they were all about. So yes, let's tell him the next time we see him—and soon. There is something else, though." He told her about his nightmare while he was sleeping in the sun.

She blinked at him.

"None of the others is having these dreams, so maybe there's nothing to them. Then maybe there is. We should tell Surston about the other dreams first and go from there."

CHAPTER THIRTY-ONE

The Dream

Not long after Ewan mentioned his first dreams to Avril, he told Surston with Avril present. He had written them down at Avril's insistence because they were so strange.

"Ah," said Surston, "this is truly interesting. Now I see what your involvement amounts to, I think. I knew it would be revealed to me sometime. It seems you might be related to the traveler."

"Me? But how?"

"You have inherited his experiences through hereditary memory," said Surston.

"You mean, he's my ancestor and I remember his life and stories through my dreams?"

"Yes, something like that," said Surston. "It may be more than that. His name was Gorvic. He has a story that covers different times, mysterious, and powerful ancients of whom he was one and those ancients, who still exist today, may be part of you. Your help may be needed even to this day. You are of their blood, then, and maybe there is a need for concern here."

He seemed to be thinking aloud to himself.

"We must find out exactly what powers that might be...well...leave it with me. I don't mean to alarm you. It may be nothing.

"You see," said Surston, "there are several people involved here. The old king was a good man, Oscarlin. Someone once wrote this of him:

I cannot say, and I will not say that he is dead; he is just away.

With a smile on his face and a wave of his hand,

He has wandered to that better land and left us dreaming.

How very fair its needs must be, since he lingers there.

I cannot say, and I will not say that he is dead; He is just away."

"Oh," said Avril, "that's from an old poem by James Whitcomb Riley."

"How well read you are Avril, but I think you're right. It certainly applies to the good King Oscarlin." Surston continued, "His elder son was Prince Lairg, and the younger was Prince Darvol. Each had loyal thanes or Lords who stood by their princes when all should have been loyal to the cause of the common good. But Prince Darvol had planted seeds of discontent long before his father, King Oscarlin, had died or moved on. The population had been increasing in the land, and although there was no immediate problems, Prince Darvol had painted a picture of gloom for the future under his brother, Prince Lairg. When the showdown erupted, much to the surprise of the new King Lairg, it was too late to defend his part of the country, and he retreated to a mountain cave. That was where he met with the Tuftefolk, who were actually a branch of a greater population of tribesmen known as the Hulderfolk. The Hulderfolk were called the hidden ones because they lived underground, while the Tuftefolk often liked to stay above. They were little folk. There was another branch of the tribe called the Sveltfolk, who liked the water as their habitat. Do you follow me, Ewan?"

"Well, yes, it's not complicated yet, but when was this all taking place?"

"Several centuries ago, thousands of years ago, but understand that time is unimportant. There have been many evil times from long ago and more yet to come. The most recent was the war just passed."

"Perhaps they have passed for now," Ewan said.

"I would tell you if that were true, but I fear not," Surston said solemnly.

"Tell me more about the meaning of the dream."

Chapter Thirty-One

"Ah, yes, well here is the story. Back to a time before even I existed. Hmm. On thinking again, I would prefer to wait awhile so I can think on this, then perhaps we'll meet in a nice secluded place away from prying ears. I've always had a fondness for the cairn by the Corlic and to the wee teahouse barn yonder. Let's do that. But to hear the story as it was later told of the traveler, I think the others should also hear it. We will plan that for a later time."

CHAPTER THIRTY-TWO

The Teahouse and the Amulets

It was quite some time before Surston decided to meet again, or so it seemed to Ewan and Avril, but at last here they were on a bright warm day at the Corlic overlooking the Clyde Valley in a wee patch of mist surrounding the base of the cairn. Surston changed his shape from his real image to a shepherd this time.

"What now?" asked Ewan.

"Well, I think the teahouse would be a fine place to be about now. I sensed you are both hungry. Maybe we can find refreshments. It's a short walk. It's early, and there's lots of time to talk more about Gorvic's journey."

With that, he rose and started toward the teahouse with Ewan and Avril in total agreement. The farm that hosted the teahouse was one of the most charming spots in the area. Where the cairn itself was the highest spot in the parish, the farm seemed as if it could have been the most hidden, yet it was not hard to find. It may have been part of one of the old Roman roads that passed through the center of it. The road ran straight through most farms, but up here in the hills it was all local traffic, mostly neighboring farmers. But the teahouse was an attraction to outside visitors, hikers mostly. Farm buildings stood on both sides of the road, although the main farmhouse was opposite and north of the teahouse. Just behind the teahouse was a stream of fresh clear water, one of many in these hills. Nearby was the underground tunnel from the Gryfe Reservoir to Greenock, although it was believed to be connected to many Faerie tunnels underneath. If the truth be known, it was indeed.

For Avril, this was the first time visiting the teahouse. Chickens and geese pecked around on both sides of the road. A dog, which sat curiously watching them from the front door of the main house, suddenly rose. Tail wagging, it ran over to Surston and licked his hand. The dog looked around as if searching for another dog. On seeing none, it walked back to the doorstep and sat down again. Two cats, one ginger and one black, sprawled just outside the door of the barn and showed no great interest in the visitors. Ewan pulled a couple of times on the rope of a small bell hanging on the branch of an old oak tree. The teahouse was, in essence, an old barn, rectangular with a few windows added for more sunlight. A few tables of various shapes and sizes were spread throughout, with about four chairs around each table. Hardly one matched another. On busy weekends, the tables were ready with sugar bowls and milk jugs. Today, the tables were empty. Ewan was glad to be sharing with just Surston and Avril without strangers around so they could talk, although he was eager to share these goings-on with the rest of the Cruach. Surston hesitated. His eyes narrowed.

"This is not really a good place to go into the rest of Gorvic's journey," he said.

"You're right about that," Avril said as they peered around, "but I don't think we are in any harm. There is something or somebody here who is just nosy."

"Indeed, I think you're right," said Surston, "but I'd prefer to wait."

"What is it?" asked Ewan.

"Just a Brownie somewhere," said Avril.

A door opened at the main farmhouse, and a sturdy, buxom woman of about fifty and about five foot eight strode across the path carrying a tray with a teapot and cups. She had black hair with some gray fighting to show through, but she held an air of youth about her. She was followed by a girl of eight or so with clear similarities that identified her as the daughter. She smiled at Ewan and was obviously pleased to see him. After they set down the trays, the girl had an inclination to stay, but her mother said, "Come away now, child."

"Och, Mum," protested the lass.

Ewan, sensing her wish for company, said, "I'll stop by outside for a while when we've finished our tea."

"OK," said the lass. "I've got something to show you, Ewan. My name's Fiona."

"Fiona what?" asked Ewan.

"Fiona Fraser." Without looking at Avril or Surston, she skipped away and across to the house. Ewan sensed Avril staring at him, but he resisted returning the look until Avril forced him to. She was smiling at him.

"What?" he said.

"Oh, nothing, but how did she know your name?"

Ewan shrugged.

Surston drummed his fingers on the table.

"I think I prefer to wait for another time. There is no rush. Drink some tea, and those scones look good."

After half an hour or so, they decided it was time to leave and wandered into the yard space outside the teahouse on the side of the road. The lady came out for payment, and Avril did the honors. Ewan crossed over to talk to Fiona. Surston, Avril, and the lady were chatting. It was indeed a choice spot snuggled between hillocks with heather topping the upper slopes, trees spaced well around the farm itself, and the wee burn running down one side.

The young lady had put a necklace of sorts around Ewan's neck. After a few minutes, the lady and her daughter waved the trio good-bye. Once out

Chapter Thirty-Two

of sight of the teahouse, Surston chose to be about other business. He was gone in a gust of wind. Avril and Ewan walked a brisk pace talking about nothing in particular. Ewan was relating a time when he and Graham were playing in the heather nearby when Graham knelt on an anthill. He was bitten severely hundreds of times. His knee swelled up, and Ewan thought he'd better suck out the poison. Avril interrupted.

"What did she give you?"

"What?" asked Ewan.

"That thing around your neck."

Ewan knew she wasn't jealous or anything like that but just being nosy. He felt embarrassed that Fiona appeared to have a crush on him.

"Och, don't worry about it. It's not like I'm teasing you, is it? It just shows you're a nice person, that's all."

Ewan blushed.

"Well, let me see it," she said. Ewan showed her a stone the size of a penny encased in a sort of metal cage with a leather thong strung through it, long enough to put over his head and hang around his neck. Avril noticed it was multicolored but appeared to be changing hues. It also looked oddly like an eyeball every now and then.

"Where did she get this?" Avril asked with a note of concern in her voice.

"Why?"

"It's Fae," she said.

"Fae? What does that mean? Why is everything Fae now? It's just a stone."

"No, it's an amulet. Take it off," Avril demanded.

"Why?"

"Just take it off, now!"

Ewan took off the necklace and let it drop to the grass.

"Where did she get this?" Avril asked.

"Why? What is it?"

"I'm not sure, but it's not an ordinary coloured stone. Like I said, it's an amulet. It has an aura about it. It's from deep in the earth, that I do know."

"How could you know that, and, well, wouldn't any stone possibly come from deep in the earth? I mean, it looks like the stones they make Highland jewelry with, and they have to dig that stuff up and polish it and stuff, don't they?"

"Yes, but this stone, I feel…is…I can't explain it. Didn't she tell you where she got it?"

"Not really, but she did say she has more of them."

"She does? I know what—instead of going back to ask her, and she may not know anyway, we can ask Rankle or Woody or perhaps the Heather Pixies going past the Beasy."

It was midafternoon. Ewan and Avril stopped at a burn that ran into the dam when Ewan and others had fished for minnows. Ewan sat on a rock and managed to get a message to Winthrop, hence to the heather Pixies and Woody and Rankle, the Urisks. Once the excitement of the Pixies had settled and Avril got over her shock at the Urisks' appearance once more, things settled down to matters at hand. The stone was displayed at arm's length, dangling on the leather thong. Avril insisted that the Pixies and Urisks not be in plain view of the stone. Upon seeing it, they came out of hiding and approached it with a kind of reverence, both the Urisks and the Moor Pixies.

Rankle viewed it and said, "Och, it's just a wee amulet. It protects its owner from danger or harm. It contains certain magical powers that could provide good luck for the possessor or possibly offer protection from evil or harm. It represents positive universal forces that are in exact harmony with those you wish to attract, and the more exact the symbolism, the easier it is to attract the force."

"What does that last part mean?" Ewan asked.

"Och, it just means it's good, doesn't it, Rankle?" Avril said.

"Yes, it does. There are more than two of these stones; we have some in our possession also. You must find more. They will do much good. Do you know what you have?" said Rankle.

"Not really," said Ewan.

"I think Fiona does, sort of. She's waiting to talk to you. Hold the stone in front of you and look into it," said Rankle.

Chapter Thirty-Two

Ewan was surprised to see an image of Fiona at what he thought at first was just a picture.

"Hello, Ewan," Fiona said as her image smiled back at him from the stone. "I knew you would figure it out. It's wonderful, isn't it?"

"It is indeed," said Ewan, "but is this really you?"

"It is indeed," she said. "It's a bit of Faerie magic."

"But I need to know where you got it. This is very important."

"Aye, I got it from the tinkers," said Fiona.

"Don't tell me now. Others may be listening, and Avril is a little bit nervous about it. I will come there soon but not today, maybe tomorrow, and you can tell me all about it."

"OK, I'm always around the farm here," she said.

Turning to the others, Ewan said, "I can contact you through this stone, and the ones that you and the Pixies have, but I need to spend some time with her alone. I don't want to alarm her."

The next day, Ewan left Avril with the Pixies and Urisks at the Beath Dam awaiting his call while he went to meet Fiona at the cairn. White clouds flew across the skies as Ewan waited for Fiona. Looking out to view the Clyde and turning to the hills behind him, he thought how he loved it up there. There was no threat of rain, and the wind, although brisk, was not cold. He sat with his back against the cairn, which rose to a height of about twelve feet and was broad at the base. He wondered how long it had been here, who put the first stone, and how many and why, and how the area known as Corlic got its name. He could have drifted off into a dream despite the rock mattress at his back when he heard a soft "Hello."

"Oh, hello," he said.

"Isn't this just a great place?" said Fiona.

"It is that," replied Ewan. "You're lucky to live here, so quiet mostly. Are ye bothered by the hikers who visit here?"

"Och no, not really. It's no' that troublesome. In fact, ye can meet some interesting people sometimes."

"Aye well, I could do with more of that," Ewan said sarcastically.

"What?" asked Fiona.

"Oh, nothing. It's just that I've been meeting quite a few interesting people recently."

"I see. So where's your stone?"

"It's safe around my neck. Now that you mention it, that's what I want to talk to you about. When you gave it to me, you didn't tell me about it or what it was."

"That's because when the wee tinker lassie gave them tae me she didnae tell me anything either. I just found out, and I thought that's the way they worked."

"What wee tinker lassie, and how many did she give you?" asked Ewan.

"Just the two, but she's got more. I saw them."

"And who is she?"

"Oh, she comes by every so often. She's the same age as I. She only comes when it's misty like, you ken?"

"This is important," said Ewan, "all right? She's with a family with a wee horse and cart, and her brothers play the bagpipes and have the Gaelic tongue as well as English."

"Oh well, you've met her then."

"Aye, a couple times at the back of the loch. How many times have you met them?"

Fiona thought for a moment. "I've seen them over maybe two years, but they come by only once in a while. I speak to them through the stones a lot."

"Wait a minute," said Ewan. "Do you mind if I bring in Avril? You remember her?"

"Of course I do. She's been sitting at the bottom of the road wi' the Pixies and yon other things."

Fiona waved, and Avril waved back. Ewan motioned for them to come up. In two seconds, they were all standing in front of Ewan and Fiona.

"How did you get here so fast from the dam? Oh, don't bother, as if I don't know at this point," said Ewan.

"We just hitched on tae a wee breeze," Avril said with a laugh. "And we've already talked to Fiona through the Urisks' stones, handy things these. That's why we're here, though. It's the stones, which brings up the subject of the tinkers you met in the mist. You didn't tell me about them."

"Och, I'm sure you knew anyway. You're always a bit ahead of the rest of us. Tell me, seeing you always seem to know, does Fiona have the gift?" asked Ewan.

"No," said Avril, "even though she's had all this contact—the house Brownie, the tinkers, the mist, and everything. This is just a heavy Fae area, and the family is liked by them."

"But will that not put her in harm's way?"

"It wouldn't have, but with having a stone now, I don't know."

This wee conversation was on the side with Ewan and Avril, while Fiona chatted with the others.

"But she's talking to the Faeries. How can she do that?" asked Ewan.

"I don't know. Another question for Winthrop, I think."

"Could you take it away and put a forgetting spell on her, if there is such a thing?" mused Ewan.

"Yes, but her tinker friend will ask her about it and maybe give her another, if she has any more, and I believe she does. We have to visit the land of the mist, Ewan. I know you've been avoiding that, although you've been there. You must go in. We all must, and we must locate some other stones. I wonder how the tinkers came upon them."

"And I wonder, too, just exactly how they work," said Ewan.

"Goff will know more now, I hope. I wonder if she is here. We need to do this away from Fiona," said Avril.

They turned back to the rest just as laughter was being spread around. As ugly as the Urisks were, their laughing was magic to the ears, a combination of gurgling, bubbling, hiccups, ha-ha-ha, and hee-hee-hee. It was dangerous to get them started because it was hard to stop laughing while they were. The Heather Pixies, or Moor Pixies, were enjoying the company of Landerfolk more and more each time. Ewan and Avril decided to stay longer. They kept their talk lighthearted with Fiona present. Ewan remembered he could mind-talk with them, without Fiona's knowledge.

"This Faerieland," thought Ewan, "when you are not in our world, what is it like?"

"Ah, it is dedicated mostly to our pleasure," said Goff. "We like music and dance; we like good food and drink. Many of these things we like in variety. That is why we sometimes borrow from this world. The pipes and the fiddle are most in demand. Sometimes, though, we overextend the visits of our chosen friends, and if they wish to return to their own worlds, we cannot stop them. But the problem is Faerie time is not like your time. A night with us can sometimes be a hundred years with you. Upon return, Landerfolk age and shrivel to dust. Sometimes we trick them and they stay with us forever. They play their fiddles and pipes for us and become our Faerie musicians. We look after them well. There are ways to return them to their proper time, but we most often do not do that. It is regrettable, but some of our Faerie folk are not always fair, so to speak. While here, though, we keep them happy with our food and Faerie drink. Understand that the Pixies and Faeries are not always in agreement with treatment of folk from your world."

"I have heard stories of Faerie pipers and fiddlers," said Ewan, "and of your food and drink. The land of the mists—is that part of Faerieland?"

"It is, but there we can overrule the time elements. It is sort of in be-tween. I sense that that is why you show a reluctance to visit again. There is no danger to Fiona when we allow her in. Some choose to stay if we wish them to. Your...er...grand-uncles enjoy the heather ale and Faerie whiskey," he said.

"You have seen them? You know them?"

"Why, yes," said Goff. "They enjoy the quieter spots behind the mists. They are your favorite spots too."

"Really? You mean all my camping and hiking spots are where my great-uncles are?"

"That's true," said Goff.

"Why do they never return?" asked Ewan.

"They used to, but after those of their generation passed on, it was lonely. They have each other, though, as well as others. But one of your uncles, well, he likes solitude."

"I've heard that he does. So I should visit again. I would like to and, yes, I will. I met the tinkers that Fiona knows. Did you know that?"

Chapter Thirty-Two

Goff nodded without speaking. All this was among Avril, Ewan, and Goff through mind talk. Suddenly, a voice said, "A penny for your thoughts." Fiona walked over to Ewan.

"I was just saying…oh, nothing. I was just daydreaming."

"It's easy to do that up here," said Fiona.

"Are we any closer to finding more stones?"

"We will be soon," said Fiona. "While you were daydreaming, I contacted the McLeans. They are the tinkers, and they call themselves traveling people. They are kin to the folks at McLean's farm, at Garvock near the island."

Avril said, "Ewan knows them. He met them a time or two. We can gather with them whenever we wish. They are now somewhere near Auchinbreck, west of Dunoon. They can take the mists to be here. When Goff summons us all, we will come. I hope soon we can all have a stone, and I will look forward to contacting the others. There are some adventures for us."

"What about Fiona?" Ewan said aside to Avril.

"We'll have to bide awhile, won't we, now?"

Meanwhile, Surston and Winthrop had been deciphering Ewan's dream but hesitated in explaining it. Mr. Gillanders had been traveling on his lecture tour and was due back soon, and Surston wanted him to be present for the discussion.

CHAPTER THIRTY-THREE

The Seelie Court

BEFORE SURSTON AND Winthrop could meet with Mr. Gillanders, the Seelie Court stepped in, in a dramatic and unexpected way. It was a cold and misty day behind Loch Thom, and the mist was one of the Seelie Court's bidding. Surston, Winthrop, and Mr. Gillanders found themselves summoned along with all the members of the Cruach by the big Faeries, the Seelie Court. Three of them were there to greet them. There they stood, six feet tall or more with flowing white hair falling almost to their waists, pale and translucent white-skinned hands and faces. They were draped in garments that made them seem more graceful than any Landerfolk—long white robes that covered them from their shoulders to their feet with only their faces and hands uncovered. Their eyes were large and oblong without pupils, and their ears were long and pointed. It was difficult to tell whether they were male or female, so graceful were they.

Behind them were three large spherical objects resembling large soap bubbles, each like a ten-by-ten-foot room, only round. They had no visible openings.

The first to speak was Mr. Gillanders. Turning first to the children, he said, "I'm sure there is no reason for alarm. Don't be afraid."

Turning to Surston and Winthrop, he asked, "What is this all about? I'm sure we were all in the middle of something, and all of a sudden we disappear. There will be questions."

Winthrop was about to say something when Surston raised his hand.

"You will not be missed. As soon as this meeting is over, and I'm sure there is no harm here, we will be returned to exactly the same time and place we have just been taken from. Am I right, sirs?" he asked the big Faeries.

When the big Faeries spoke, it was not exactly in voices, but as Mr. Gillanders recalled from the Reverend Robert Kirk's diary, they sounded *like bells chiming and flutes blowing sweet melodies.* The sound was immediately soothing and reassuring to all present, though not altogether unfamiliar to Surston and Winthrop.

"You know we mean you no harm, and you also knew, Surston, that it would come to this. This enchanting collection of children was brought together by us and with the help of Avril's mother."

Although not many outside this group would have understood these angelic voices with their ever light and musical tones, everybody present did.

Ewan tried to say something but mumbled without getting out anything intelligent.

"Oh, my dear child, speak as you have been speaking to the Earth Faeries before now. We are not that much different. You can relax with us," said one of them.

Brian, who was more forward than the rest, said, "Do you know all of our names, and do you have names, and what are those big round things behind you?"

That was an icebreaker. Immediately, everybody started talking about the big round things, what they were made of, what their names were, and whether they could touch their robes.

"Our names...well, as long as you can tell us apart, I will give you our names in your own way of speaking so you can understand. I am Aab." Turning toward the others, he said, "This is Bea, and this is Crom."

Bea and Crom bowed slightly toward everybody.

"Ah, the big round things. Well, they are...how should we describe them? They are space vessels...or perhaps a chariot is a better word. Would you like to ride in them?"

"Yes, yes, I would." They all chimed in except Mr. Gillanders, who cautiously said, "They look like soap bubbles. Will they pop?"

"They are made of Sii. It is something that you will not find here on Earth. It will not pop. It is made of a strong material that would be more precious than gold or diamonds if it were found on Earth. We control these vessels with our minds, and they can carry us faster than the speed of light," said Crom.

Mr. Gillanders was recalling his first conversation with Surston and glanced toward him. These were the visitors from other worlds, but they could not return, and here they were.

"So are we ready to take a trip among the stars? It seems so. We will go in three separate chariots, so we need to divide into groups," said Crom.

Ewan, Avril, Mr. Gillanders, and Surston were selected to go with Aab. Bea took Winthrop, Belle, Brian, Billy, and Shauna. The last group consisted of Leslie, Graham, Pauline, and Crom.

"How do we get into them?" asked Pauline. "There's no door or anything." Before her next thought, everybody was snug inside on invisible but comfortable seats.

"Well, let's go," Crom said. In a flash, they were deep in space looking around at some of the most amazing sights and colours imaginable.

Mr. Gillanders was nervous but tried not to show it while the children, being children, seemed to view it as a carnival ride at the fair.

They show no fear. Perhaps this is why they, in particular, have been chosen for this—whatever it is—but why me?

Chapter Thirty-Three

Your own curiosity and your contact with the Reverend Kirk, that's why. Mr. Gillanders was aware that Surston was reading his thoughts.

I feel your apprehension, but don't worry. I've blocked your thoughts for now to just ourselves. Relax and enjoy; you are in no harm's way. I have been here many times before.

They were dangling in outer space with nothing but a thin film of Sii below them, above them, and around them. Stars and planets loomed everywhere, and colours more brilliant than any rainbow flashed out of nowhere from every direction. The vessels were all close together so everybody could see one another and talk and wave. The Cruach pointed and asked questions all at once until Bea raised his long, skinny finger and said, "There is your Mother Earth."

It's so small. How far away are we?" asked Leslie.

"A great distance, yet we are even farther away from our own home from whence our people once came."

The sounds of the voices of the Seelie Court were still like music, but it did rise and fall like happy and sad songs.

"You mean that you don't live on Earth...or didn't live on Earth? Where is...or where was your home? Where is it now?" asked Brian.

Just as the others were about to start a barrage of questions, Aab took over the situation by focusing on the minds of all present. Some in the party knew the story, but for the Cruach and most others, this was new. Aab told them that many years ago their home planet was becoming inhabitable from devastating wars so they had to find a new place to live. They had great ships that could travel to other worlds. When they found a place to start anew, they moved their people. When they arrived on Earth, others had already arrived from other worlds. Great wars took place for a good many years with the other visitors and Earth beings until finally some order took place.

"We made a fine alliance with your Earth Faeries and became...well... big Faeries and...they...the little Faeries to most Landerfolk. Now we live in what we like to call the Realm of the Fae. It's like another dimension, but right here on Earth, or should I say right there on Earth, above and beneath, in mountains, caves, and deep down including the seas," said Aab.

"There are many different kinds of us, as you have been told. Some good, some bad. Different shapes and sizes, some akin to animals, others more Landerfolk-like, and others more in spirit form."

While floating or traveling among planets and suns and meteors, the Cruach with Mr. Gillanders remained silent but thinking. It didn't take long before the silence was broken with questions all at once, but the most important to all was, "Can we visit the Realm of the Fae?"

Suddenly, there was darkness. It was so black in an instant that not anyone could think. All awareness was gone. No thoughts could be read. Just how long it stayed like that, no one knew—at least none of the Cruach or Mr. Gillanders. But really it had been only a split second since they traveled through space to this place of darkness. Then, from far away, a pinprick of light appeared. It started to grow, and awareness crept back into the minds of the Cruach and Mr.Gillanders. They were no longer in the space chariots but seated cross-legged in a line, all facing this light. Fear gripped them all for the first time, and they held hands tightly with those next to them. As the light gradually grew, easiness came over everybody. It was like a rising sun now, the air getting warmer and more cheerful. The light was no longer a pinprick but a glowing sphere that suddenly disappeared and left the company in a world not unlike their own with fields and trees, with streams running down small hills into ponds. The small hills disappeared into mountains in the distance. But this was not their world as they knew it; this was part of the Realm of the Fae. As they all got to their feet to look around, they noticed just how tall the Seelie Court beings were—or was it that they floated above the ground now and that made them look taller?

"Where are we really?" The question was on the minds of all, or at least the Cruach and the minister.

"Let me explain," said Aab. "Our realm is really like a parallel world to yours, a different dimension. I'll try to make it simple. Imagine two big huge buildings with lots of different creatures and beings living in each one. One is your world—Earth, as you call it—and the other is ours, the Realm of the Fae. There are ways to go from one to the other, but it's not as easy to do for one population as it is for the other. There are certain

Chapter Thirty-Three

doorways, or portals, that lead to the land between the buildings, and they allow travel between the buildings. But from your Earth building, these doorways are not easy to find or to use.

"The Realm of the Fae contains many wonders, and although it may appear similar to your Earth, in many ways it is very different from your world."

CHAPTER THIRTY-FOUR

Looking Forward

Just like that, the visit was over. They were all back in the cold mists of the hills behind Greenock. It was almost like it had never happened. It went so quickly that everyone was back to where they had been. That is, except Surston, Winthrop, Aab, Bea, and Crom.

"Surston, Winthrop, listen," said Crom. "The Cruach could be in harm's way. They are certainly being used. But by whom, we are not quite sure, although we do have our suspicions. When we came to your Earth thousands of years ago, we did come with other visitors. After many wars and conflicts, we managed some sort of peace and, realizing the improbability of returning to our own worlds, we had to hide our vessels, our ships, along with the vast knowledge and technologies we brought with us. Earth's people were not ready for such things. Over the years, we have released some of this knowledge to mankind in the hopes they would use it to their advantage, and for the most part they have.

"We shared some of this with your more responsible Earth Faeries, with both the little ones and the spirit Faeries who have a more superior knowledge than some of the others. There are many, of course, in this race, some with similar spiritual qualities as ourselves. Many others have been welcomed to our spirit realm and become such as we are, for we were once the same."

"I'm beginning to understand now, but you have hidden so much from even us for so many years," said Surston.

"It was for your own safety, my dear friend. For as long as we fought for peaceful solutions, there were some who did not agree to our terms. They have been in search of our ships. But we have hidden them in a part of our realm, where they will never find them. They are trying, through the Cruach, to find them."

"But by taking the Cruach into your realm, did you not expose yourselves somewhat?" asked Winthrop.

"Not so. Our realm is vast, and where we took you was not remotely near our secrets. But as we hope, if it entices whomever we think, we will know who they are and act accordingly," said Bea. "You know us as the Seelie Court, and we are friendlier to you. Our counterparts, the Unseelie Court, do not trust others of a different realm and so are not as readily approached, and they guard our secrets."

"So there we have it," said Surston. "It appears as though we will now be asked to be more alert in the future. And what of Mr. Gillanders?"

"We will watch over him as we will the Cruach."

"You say the Cruach are in danger. Is this the truth?"

"Of course, but let them continue to have their fun. I would not yet think they are in any immediate danger, but they are having quite an adventure and are aware of the challenges ahead. They are well on their way to being protected by their Faerie partners, and we will make sure that Belle, Brian, and Billy are safe and will soon be introduced to their partners. One day, they may not remember any of this, but for now, let's wait and see what the future brings."

Surston and Winthrop were left alone to wait and watch and wonder. What would the future bring?

To be continued…

About the Author

Carl R. Peterson spent his early life in Greenock, Scotland, where he was born to a Nordic Scot, his mixed heritage of Swedish and Scottish Highlander having carried through the generations.

Musically inclined, Peterson enjoyed a successful folk and rock music career in Canada, releasing twenty-five recordings through the years. One folk group, The Patmacs, was featured on several Canadian TV shows, and The King Beezz, his rock group, was considered part of the British Invasion, touring nationally.

He has also enjoyed solo musical success in both Canada and the United States. One of his albums, *Scotland Remembers the Alamo*, and its companion book, *Now's the Day and Now's the Hour*, sparked his interest in writing, prompting his creation of *Ewan Colin Coupar and a Touch of the Fae*.

Peterson also enjoys keeping fit by jogging and orienteering as well as engaging in leisure activities like golf, sailing, and kayaking.

CPSIA information can be obtained
at www.ICGtesting.com
Printed in the USA
LVOW13s1136190217

524727LV00009B/710/P